MW01679872

A THRIFT SHOP MURDER

CATS, GHOSTS AND AVOCADO TOAST - BOOK 1

L.C. HIBBETT
N.M. HOWELL

Crawford County Library District
Bourbon • Cuba • Steelville

Cover by
DAQRI BERNARDO OF COVERS BY COMBS
Proof by
CP BIALOIS

DUNGEON MEDIA

CHAPTER ONE

One, two, three. I counted slowly as I inhaled and exhaled. *Peace and Zen,* I chanted internally. *Peace and Zen.* Keep it together, Price. You are a calm, confident woman who can master life's curve balls.

"Stuff your pie holes, you saggy old bats!"

I raised a hand to my mouth and squeezed my lips together to muffle my snort of nervous laughter as the old woman to my left began a fresh tirade of abuse. The surrounding mourners did not even glance over their shoulders as the woman muttered about wrinkly fartbags and hairy chins. Obviously, angry-shouting-lady was a neighborhood regular; trust me to stand next to the loopiest person at the memorial service.

The wind chilled my skin and I tugged my cardigan tighter around myself; my wardrobe choice was ill-planned for an outdoor event so early in the spring. Not that I had planned to be standing in the middle of a public park attending a stranger's funeral, mind you. No, my plan had been to dump my bags in my new apartment, soak in a hot bath while I downed a bottle of Salem's finest organic red wine, and sleep for four solid days until starting my new job. Clearly, fate had other plans. Stupid fate. Stupid life.

Please proceed to the memorial in the park by the river for further instruction.

I read the note I had found pinned to the door of my new apartment for the tenth time and scanned the small gathering for any sign of my new landlord. I had only ever spoken to the woman on the phone, and briefly at that, so all I knew was that I was looking for an older lady.

Standing on my tip toes, I peered over the heads of those in front of me, searching for any sign of my new landlord and boss. A small man in black robes and a white collar teetered on top of a milk crate as he read the eulogy from what appeared to be the back of a shopping receipt. He raised his voice to be heard over the sound of two old women squabbling like demonic school girls in the front row. Maybe one of the ladies was who I was looking for? I crossed my fingers and hoped it was the woman with the laughter lines around her eyes, not the one who looked like she was sucking on a whole bag of lemons.

"New in town?" A voice called from behind me, the

words muffled by the wind. I dropped back down on my heels and turned toward the source of the greeting, grateful for a distraction from the bizarre ceremony. I stepped back from the crowd, turning toward the stranger. The woman wore a knitted hat and a thick winter jacket with a white lab coat peeking out the bottom. She was tall and her hair was cropped short around her face to reveal high cheekbones. She gave me a warm smile. "I don't think I've seen you around here before, not from around here?"

"That obvious?" I asked. The woman laughed. "Yeah, I just moved here from Portland. It's my first day in town, actually."

The woman raised her eyebrows. "And you ended up at a memorial? Yikes. Did you know the deceased?"

"No, I didn't." I grimaced. "It's a bit awkward actually, I'm just picking up the keys to my new place and I was told to come here. I'm assuming my landlord is around here somewhere, but I haven't found her yet." I looked around at the strange assortment of mourners, ranging from elegant women with silver hair to a stunning young man wearing a pink fedora and a lime green skirt. There were no photographs beside the coffin to give any indication of who had died. "Lots of people paying their respects this afternoon; seems like a pretty tight-knit community?"

"Oh yeah, you bet it is." The woman chuckled softly. "Welcome to Salem, by the way. You'll just love it here; it's a great place to live." She held out a slim hand. "My name is Tracy. I'm sorry your introduction to our neighborhood had to be this… grim."

"Price Jones, pleased to meet you." I returned her handshake with a smile. "And trust me, a funeral is one of the nicer ways I've spent my time lately."

Tracy grimaced. "That doesn't sound great." She nodded at the bright green trees and the sparkling water. "Well, I hope you enjoy living in Salem; it's a little different from Portland."

"Different is exactly what I want right now," I said.

Tracy opened her mouth to respond but was distracted by an outburst from the top of the crowd. It was the lemon-sucking old lady. "Oh, please. What a load of claptrap; she didn't even like children. She called them hairless monkeys."

The tall, slim woman's words carried over the crowd as though she was standing on a stage. The plump, pretty lady next to her wrung her hands together and began to whisper something, but the flustered-looking priest shushed the two old women, clearly aggrieved by the interruption to his praise of the deceased's kindness to the local children. The taller woman dismissed him with a wave of her hand and continued to bicker with her companion. "Don't be ridiculous, Dot. You know she thought they were filthy and smelly."

I tried to focus on the eulogy, but the sheer disregard of the old women and for the nature of the event made for compelling viewing. You didn't see old women placing bets and throwing insults at the funerals in Hillsdale. Unfortunately.

"Boo hoo! As if you two have ever done anything decent, you withered old prunes." Oh, man. The raised voices had provoked the tiny old woman to my left again, and she fumed as she glared at the chattering ladies, her eyes wild and her expression somewhere between menacing and hysterical. She turned to me and huffed. "Can you believe those cows? What utter witches. A pair of scagbags, that's what they are."

Don't laugh, Price. It's a funeral and these are your new neighbors. I offered the woman an apologetic grimace and sucked in a slow breath. *Deep breath in. Hold for three seconds. Slow and steady breath out.* I was a major self-help geek and had learned the calming technique from one of my favorite holistic wellness podcasts created by my idol, Dr. Lee. I had found myself practicing it at least a dozen times a day over the past weeks, but not usually to stop me from collapsing into hysterical laughter. That was a first.

Tracy leaned closer to me as if sensing my discomfort. She nodded toward where lemon-sucker and her friend were engaging in a full-blown argument. "Don't worry, not everyone in Salem is that crazy. I promise."

My lips curved as I looked at the two old women. The priest's face was a deep shade of purple as he glared at them over his crumpled piece of paper and it looked as though he was on the verge of an aneurysm, but the ladies didn't appear to be planning to relent any time soon.

"Who are those two women?" I asked, turning my back to the grumbling lady beside me.

"Dot Murphy and Bianca D'Arcy," Tracy said. "Local celebrities in their own right, or so they'd have you believe. You'll be seeing a lot of them in town. Dot is pretty sweet, but Bianca is something entirely different, I'm afraid. That woman has a core of steel and a tongue like a whip."

"As I was saying…" The priest cleared his throat and began shouting at the top of his lungs, his cheeks flushed and his voice hoarse. "The deceased…"

"So, Price?" Tracy's voice pulled my attention away from the increasingly high-pitched man. "Who did you say your landlord was?"

As if on cue, both the priest and I spoke in unison, "Agatha Bentley."

I blanched and stared at the priest. After a long moment, and with a dry mouth, I managed to whisper, "What did he just say?"

"Oh, Price. I'm so sorry," Tracy said. "But this is Mrs. Bentley's funeral." She placed a steadying hand on my shoulder, concern in her eyes. "Darn it, somebody should have told you. Are you all right?"

No. I was very much not all right. I was no-place-to-live, no-job-to-go-to, fiancé-kicked-me-out-on-my-ass, too-proud-to-beg-one-of-my-not-so-interested-parents-to-take-me-in not all right. Shoot, shoot, shoot. I took a deep breath and lifted my chin with a smile. "Of course, I'm great, thank you. Just a little surprised."

The ceremony ended to the sharp applause of the taller of the two irreverent old women and the continued grumbling of the third old woman beside me. The crowd dispersed before I had a chance to realize what was going on and I got the sneaking suspicion that most of the people had attended out of obligation, not love. Perhaps Agatha Bentley hadn't been all that well-liked in the community. Maybe she wasn't a very nice person, and this was the universe's way of protecting me from a bad experience. I ground my teeth together and tried to convince myself the world was acting in my best interest instead of taking another gigantic poop on my already poop-stained head.

As I watched the mourners flee from the park, I felt a stab of sympathy for the deceased thrift shop owner. I wondered who would stay by my coffin if I dropped dead. My cell phone contact list was jammed to the brim, but I couldn't count a single true friend on it. Gerard, my ex-fiancé, had taken all our friends in the split, and I guessed he'd already handed them to Ivana; my friends, my bed, my life. But not my clothes. Because she had a perfect juicy butt to go with her toned tummy and her full bust. She had no need for my push-up bras or narrow leggings, so Gerard had packed those up for me and Fed-exed them with a gift hamper and a card thanking me for the seven years we'd spent together and my understanding response to his need to move on. The note was written in his secretary's handwriting. Douchebag.

I clenched my back teeth and forced myself back to the present moment to discover the crowd had almost entirely disappeared , except for the priest, leaving the coffin alone in the middle of the park. I raised my eyebrows. What a weird funeral.

Tracy hung back with me, as did the strange old lady who continued to mutter under her breath as she glared across the field at the backs of the retreating funeral guests. I was unsure whether to stick around or head back to the apartment, the note on the door had merely told me to go to the park, nothing more.

"So." Tracy turned toward me. "What are you going to do now?" I felt a swell of gratitude that I'd somehow happened upon one of the less bizarre inhabitants of downtown Salem. It offered some comfort that I at least wasn't totally alone while I headed toward the verge of a total meltdown.

"I've no idea." I shook my head. "I genuinely have no clue what I'm going to do."

"Wah, wah, wah." My head jerked back as I stared at the old woman. "You young people are always complaining," she sniped. "What could you possibly have to complain about apart from the fact that your pants are always ten sizes too tight for your weird skinny little bodies?"

My eyes grew wide as I watched the old lady roll her eyes, clearly unimpressed with the look of me. I quickly glanced down at my stretch-denim pants and frowned. "I…"

"You'll figure it out," Tracy interrupted, completely ignoring Bitchy Mc Grayhair. "I might be able to—"

"Excuse me, ladies." A tall man with a thick mustache approached, carrying a large envelope in one hand and bouquet of flowers in the other. He cut across Tracy with a respectful nod before he fixed his attention on me. "I'm the local mayor, are you Priscilla Jones?"

"Price Jones," I corrected. "And yep, that's me."

"Price," the old woman spat, her voice shrill. "What kind of a stupid name is that? Young people these days have no respect for proper names."

I waited to see how Tracy and the man would react to the old woman's insulting rant, but they stared right through her. I bit down on my lip and did my best to follow their lead. Maybe if I ignored her she'd go away? There were plenty of old people in Portland, but I'd never seen anyone quite like the three women at this funeral before.

"Price Jones, my apologies. Priscilla was written on the deeds. This is for you. Mrs. Bentley's attorney asked me to make sure you got it." The mayor handed me the envelope before turning to Tracy, his eyes bright and his smile wide. "And these are for you. I can't thank you enough for what you've done for Max. You truly are a miracle woman."

"Just doing my job, Larry. Thanks." Tracy's expression was blank as she accepted the flowers. She turned her back to him pointedly, so she faced me once more. "Everything okay, Price?"

Deeds? Did he say deeds? I peered inside the envelope and saw a series of large metal keys on a ring sitting amongst a thick stack of printed paper. I pulled out the key ring and inspected it, conscious of the furrows forming on my brow. Gerard's voice rang in my ears, reminding me that most women in their late twenties were already having Botox injections to get their complexions' fresh. As fresh as Ivana's peachy butt, probably. I pursed my lips.

"Are those Agatha's keys?" Tracy raised her eyebrows in surprise. "Well, looks like you have a place to stay, after all."

The mayor looked as if he were about to say something, but having been so clearly dismissed by Tracy, he turned and walked away from us with hunched shoulders and a downturned face. Tracy looked at her watch and cursed. "Oh crap, I'm going to be late for my next client. It was great meeting you, Price." She rummaged through her pocket and pulled out a small square business card. "Here's my card. If you need anything at all, or if you fancy grabbing a coffee, give me a call anytime. My office is just down the street from Agatha's store." She gave my shoulder a tight squeeze before turning and following the other mourners across the field.

CHAPTER TWO

I STOOD FROZEN IN PLACE AS TRACY WALKED AWAY AND tucked the card into the envelope with the other papers. The keys felt heavy in my hand, and I wrapped my fingers tightly around them, considering what I should do next. I needed to sit down and figure out what the hell was going on. I also figured I should at least go move my bags inside before someone stole them, hoping that they hadn't already. Not that I had much left to steal. In the seven years we'd been together, while I had helped him through grad school and starting his yogalates business, what had been mine, had been Gerard's. But as it turned out, what was Gerard's, was just Gerard's. Goodbye car, goodbye home, goodbye everything but my panties and my clothes. The bastard hadn't even sent on my little buzzy…friends.

A shadow moved at my side and I realized the old

lady was still there. She glared at Tracy's retreating back. "Well, I'll be, accepting flowers from the mayor, is it? I can't believe that woman has got herself another lady date already. What a hussy."

I pinched my lips and turned my back to the cranky old woman, slowly making my way across the field toward Agatha Bentley's apartment. To my dismay, the old woman followed, babbling incessantly. I increased my pace, hoping that she would get the hint, and I let out a sigh of relief when I noticed she had disappeared by the time I rounded the corner to the block the apartment was on.

Letting out a slow breath as I held the envelope the mayor had given me against my stomach, my eyes scanned the surrounding buildings. Agatha Bentley's property stood at the far end of a small commercial street directly adjacent to the park, and her apartment was above the thrift shop I was meant to begin work at on Monday. The building was sandwiched within a long row of three-story stone row houses. The architecture was beautiful, and all looked to be pretty old. Perfect for a thrift shop.

The thrift store was closed, but through the large glass windows I could see a surprisingly attractive display. Three tall mannequins stood in a row, decked out in pretty stylish attire. Nothing I would ever wear, mind you, but they did look super trendy. Whoever styled them had undeniably good taste. I leaned closer to the glass to peer inside, but couldn't see much else past the front display. Taking a step back, I looked at the front of the building, wondering which of the main doors led to the upstairs apartment.

I smiled with relief when I saw my bags were still tucked behind the solid stone balustrade; perhaps my luck was about to change. I climbed the front steps and tried the lock on the first door. It took a few attempts to figure out which one of the many keys to use, but luckily the door sprang open on the third try. I pulled my bags inside the dark space, shut the door behind me, leaned my back against the solid wood surface, and pressed the palms of my hands into my eyes. I inhaled slowly through my nose and exhaled loudly through my mouth, hating the fact that even breathing reminded me of Gerard and his stupid yogalates classes.

My muscles clenched at the thought of him, sending a pulse of rage through me. I was alone in a strange city with even stranger people, with no landlady and no boss, and who knew whether I still even had a job or not. Things had certainly taken a turn in my life, and I had to get back my control soon or risk losing it completely. I let my hands fall to my side, emitting an extremely loud and frustration-filled groan.

I jumped about a foot in the air when I heard a loud hissing sound and the back of my head slammed hard against the door. I cursed loudly, looking frantically about for the source of the sound. Hardly any light filtered in through the heavily dust-covered window, and I fumbled at the adjacent wall for a light. My fingers came to a heavy switch, and I flicked it on, nearly blinded by the brightness flooding the entryway. Squinting, I let out a soft gasp as I took in the room around me. The building was ancient, for sure, and a thick layer of dust coated every surface. Strange wall hangings adorned the faded floral-papered walls, and to my horror, three massive furry cats sat on the stairway, staring at me with expressions that looked nearly as confused as I felt.

"Perfect. Cats." I glared at the three oversized fluffy creatures. "Well, aren't you just the cherry on top of an utterly lousy day." I'd never been a cat person. I was highly allergic, for one. Plus, dogs were just so much more sociable. I never understood the draw of having housecats. They just kind of sat around, judging you. Exactly like these three seemed to be doing right now. Although, I did have to admit these were particularly cute as cats went. One ginger, one black as night, and one tabby cat, all of them huge, all of them immaculate, all of them glaring back at me with narrowed eyes. "What are you gaping at, cats?"

"I could ask you the same question, little miss tight pants," a voice responded.

For the second time in the space of five minutes I started in fright, this time pressing my body firmly back against the front door. My pulse raced, and my eyes darted around the hallway, landing on the three cats. I stared at them, wondering if I'd finally lost my mind after all. "You did not just speak to me." I pressed my hands against the cool wood. "Right?"

"No, they did not speak to you, ridiculous girl," the batty old lady from the park said as she appeared at the top of the narrow stairwell and frowned at me as if I was the crazy person in this scenario. "Now, quit talking to yourself and get your bags out of the entryway."

My mouth fell open. "What the heck are you doing here?" I demanded, shock sharpening my words. "Did you follow me from the park? You can't just follow people into their homes. And how did you even get in?"

The lady ignored me and motioned for me to follow her up the stairs and through the doorway. "This way. You can leave your bags in here."

I was beyond frustrated, but, to my surprise, I wasn't afraid. The woman was positively minuscule and I doubted she could do much harm even if she tried. I groaned and reluctantly dragged my bags up the stairs, through a narrow corridor, and into a living room that opened onto a dining room, and through an arch into an old-style kitchen. The old lady stood near the window in the dining area and peered out at passing cars on the street below. I wondered was the old lady a friend of the deceased? Perhaps, even a relative?

"Excuse me, but do you have a key? The door was locked when I got here." When the woman didn't answer, I added more slowly, "Did you know Mrs. Bentley? Was she a friend of yours? Did you come around often?" I stood there in silence waiting for an answer, but none came. Annoyance crept around the edges of my sleep-deprived brain. I plonked the envelope down on the dining room table and crossed my arms. "Look, I'm very sorry for your loss, but if you aren't going to talk to me, you really do need to leave. This isn't okay."

I couldn't quite read the old woman's expression. She stared at me a long moment and then shrugged. "Suit yourself."

As the woman walked past me, I noticed she was in her slippers. I watched her round the corner to the entry hall and listened for her exit. I didn't hear the door slam, but when I peered into the corridor; she was nowhere to be seen. I sprinted to the door and locked it before returning to the living room to open the envelope.

I sat down and rubbed my eyes, overwhelmed by the fact that I was sitting in a dead lady's apartment and had to figure out what I was going to do about employment. I hardly had any money, having invested all my savings into my juice bar back in Portland. The juice bar that had burned down only a week after Gerard had managed to get around to making sure my name was on the insurance policy. Squeezing my eyes shut tighter, I tried to force all thoughts of my past life out of my mind. I was here now, and I had to deal with the issues at hand.

Forward, not backward. That's what all the self-help podcasts said, anyways. Steadying my mind, I pulled the paper from the envelope and scanned the first page

Holy giant cucumbers.

"You've got to be kidding me?" I let the paper fall onto the table as I stared at it with wide eyes. My shaking finger traced the text on the front page, reading it three times over to make sure I understood what it said. When I was sure I wasn't seeing things, I sat back in the chair and sighed, listening to the sound of a purring cat as the tabby stalked into the room. Agatha Bentley had left everything to me. I had just inherited an apartment, a thrift shop, a second apartment in the basement, and all of her personal belongings. And her cats, it would seem. My mouth hung open as I processed what that meant. It couldn't be right, could it?

I reached for my cell phone and searched my email addresses for an old college friend who'd gone on to study law after we finished our undergrad in Women's Studies. I typed in a frantic message, sending her photographs of the documents. My cell beeped and I stared at my friends reply, incredulous. It was mine. It was all mine. Finally, when my eyes started to become dry from staring at the words for so long, I stood and faced the cats. My skin was itchy just looking at them. "I guess that means you three little monsters belong to me, now."

I sneezed, and I swear to god the tabby cat grinned.

Great, I had gained a thrift shop, but was beginning to lose my mind. Excellent. Just what I needed.

"Cat food is in the fridge." The old woman appeared in the kitchen, and I gasped. I hadn't even heard her come back in.

"Oh, come on!" I spread my arms wide.

The woman wagged her finger at me. "Don't raise your voice, young lady. I've been watching you and you don't have so many friends that you can afford to lose another one."

"You have got to leave," I said through gritted teeth. "Out, now. I'll call the cops if you don't leave this second."

The woman cackled. "As if those donut-eating buffoons would be able to do anything about it. But fine, fine. Whatever you say, little Miss Bossy."

"Thank you." I was positively shaking. The day had been overwhelming to the max, and I had no more words for her. I crossed my arms and waited for her to leave back through the door, but she waved her wrinkled hand at me, winked, and walked straight through the solid wall on the far side of the room.

My hands dropped down to my sides, and my mouth fell open. *Okay. Maybe I had, in fact, completely lost my mind.*

I took a deep breath in, held it for three seconds… and fainted.

CHAPTER THREE

I WOKE EARLY THE NEXT MORNING WITH THE COOL morning sunlight flooding in through the huge front windows, and for the briefest moment I had no idea where I was. Rubbing my eyes as I yawned, I thought back to the night before. I had fallen asleep at the mahogany dining table while re-reading the document that outlined my strange inheritance. My dining table. My inheritance.

The memory of the batty old lady came flooding back to me and I sat pressing my fingers against my temples. I was just overly stressed and overwhelmed. It had been an emotionally crushing couple of weeks and it had been over ten days since I'd properly meditated or practiced yoga. It had all been a bad dream. My mind needed some focus; that was all.

I picked up the scattered paper and ran my finger along the bold text, which outlined what had been left in my name. Agatha Bentley had left me everything she owned. It was sad, really, that she didn't have any family or anyone close to her to leave these things to. My gut feeling had been right at the service, she must have been a very lonely old lady. But to leave everything to a stranger she'd only interviewed over the phone? I stared at the date marked clearly on the papers next to her signature. She'd made the will the day I'd accepted her job offer. The day Gerard had told me he was getting engaged to Ivana and he needed me out of the pool house. Yes, the pool house. In Oregon.

I slowly pushed myself up off the high-backed dining chair and stretched my sore muscles before making my way into the main kitchen area, grabbing my backpack from the floor where I had tossed it the night before. I opened the small tub of oatmeal soaked in apple juice that I'd prepared the day before and sniffed it cautiously. I should have refrigerated it, but with all the mess I had not even begun to unpack. I shrugged my shoulders; it would do. I looked around the kitchen for a pot to heat it in.

"Breakfast?" A deep male voice said from behind me.

I shrieked and dropped the tub of cold oatmeal all over my bare feet and the black and white linoleum floor. I looked around frantically for the source of the voice, but there was no one else in the room apart from the huge black cat. And a radio. I exhaled and patted the old style radio, twisting the knobs to ensure it was switched off. Old radio. Dodgy wiring. I could feel the prickle of a sneeze beginning to build as I met the cat's eyes. They were large and deep blue, and he looked exceptionally unimpressed.

Inhale, count to three, exhale. It's an old house, it's an old radio. I narrowed my eyes at the cat before reaching for a roll of paper towel to clean up the mess on the floor. The oatmeal was slimy between my toes and I grimaced as I tried to mop it all up.

"So what are we having now you've ruined the oatmeal?"

My eyes shot back to the large black cat. "You did *not* just speak to me." I wasn't sure if it was a question or statement, but the cat and I simply stared at each other for a long moment in silence, challenging one another. Oh, God. It wasn't the radio. There were voices in my head. That was not a good sign. I rubbed my eyes with the back of my hand as I finished mopping up the mess and dumped the empty tub into the sink.

"Has she started the breakfast?" Another voice said.

I spun around, my heart hammering in my chest. "Who's there?"

The tabby cat sauntered into the room and jumped up on the counter beside me. His tail swung back and forth slowly as he watched me. He looked impatient. Well, as impatient as a housecat could manage to look. He blinked up at me as I gripped the edge of the counter. What the hell was going on?

"I don't know, but it smells like vomit in here and I'm for sure not eating that." The massive ginger cat padded into the room and flopped himself down on the far side of the dining area, spreading out and stretching in a warm morning sunbeam.

My eyes followed him and my body froze in place. "You're not talking to me. I'm just hearing things from the stress."

The tabby cat raised his head from the countertop, his hazel eyes glowing in the daylight. "Whatever you need to tell yourself, sugar."

I squeeze my eyes shut and pressed my hands to my ears. "I'm not going crazy. I'm not going crazy. I'm not going crazy."

The tabby cat pounced from the counter and landed on the floor beside the other two cats. "What's up with this one? She's pretty, but I'm not sure she's okay in the head."

"I think she's freaking out a bit." The ginger cat examined me with eyes the color of emeralds. "She's going to hurt herself if she keeps crushing her skull like that."

The enormous black cat stalked between the other two cats with a hiss as he stared at me. "Stop!"

The word hit me like a bolt of lightning. I spun in place and sprinted through the kitchen, grabbing the keys from the dining table as I went. I shielded my view with my hands on either side of my face, focused on the door and away from the cats. I fumbled with the keys, my hands shaking, before realizing that I didn't have to unlock the door from the inside to let myself out. I pulled on the door handle, ran through the door and slammed it behind me. Running down the stairs, my fingers played with multiple keys on the keychain before coming to a stop in front of the entry door to the thrift shop on the ground level of the building. I gripped the handle tightly, closed my eyes, and sucked in a slow breath. I counted to three and let it out slowly.

Everything is fine. I'm not going crazy.

Opening my eyes, I searched for the key that matched the lock, placed it in the keyhole, and turned it. With a small click, the door unlocked, and I pulled it open as I tried to steady myself and stepped inside, locking the door behind me.

The thrift shop was a sight to behold. There were so many items crowding the cavernous space that the walls, floors, and ceiling were all hidden from view. My eyes darted from one side to the other, trying to take it all in. I had no idea what the hell I was going to do with a thrift shop, having never really worked this kind of retail before, but walking through the large space and noticing the way daylight came flooding through the glazed storefront, I realized this could be the perfect spot for a juice bar. My juice bar. My fresh start.

A small grin spread across my face as I told myself that things were finally falling into place. Maybe I'd been letting myself succumb to the pressure a bit—imagining people walking through walls and cats talking wasn't exactly normal—but sometimes it took a little shaking or jarring of life to finally find what you're looking for. And looking around the large open space that sat on a fairly busy street near the park, I realized that this was exactly what I was looking for. I could breathe new life into this old building.

I closed my eyes and imagined what it would look like with the same setup as my shop back in Portland. A wide counter spread across the rear wall, a row of stools and clusters of seating scattered around the front. Yes, I could have seating lining the storefront, looking out over the trees that lined the road. With this much sunlight coming through, I could even grow some organic greens to use in my products. It would be perfect.

A loud meow pulled me from my reverie as the tabby cat sauntered in through the back of the shop and settled himself on a beam of sunlight in front of the window. The ginger cat appeared next and began to wrestle with a swatch of material hanging over the counter. The black cat was last to approach, his eyes fixed on my face as he circled me. I eyed the three balls of fur, wondering just how they had gotten into the store when I'd locked the door.

"So, you're deciding to act like cats now, I see." I crossed my arms. All three cats raised their heads, but I noticed instead of looking at me, they were looking past me. A shiver caressed my spine, and I braced myself as I turned toward the back of the shop and found myself staring at the familiar birdlike face of the trespassing old lady.

"Of course, they're acting like cats, you dingbat. They are cats." The old lady stood behind the cash counter and tutted at me. She still wore the same strange outfit as she had the day before; layered sweaters, pants that were two inches too short, and fluffy slippers. I shook my head as I stared at her, unsure how to address the situation at this point. She was beyond reason, and I would likely have to get the cops involved.

"Can you please tell me why you're here?" I asked in my most calm voice. If she didn't leave, I would pick her up and throw her out myself. I was fit and stronger than most girls my age. Stronger than most men, even. Tossing her over my shoulder and throwing her out the front door would hardly break a sweat. The idea was tempting, I had to admit.

"What do you mean, what am I doing here? I live here." She ran her finger over the dusty surface of the table, but when I looked closer, her finger left no trail.

I raised my eyebrows as I glared at her. The whole

situation was exceptionally odd. "I'm sorry, what did you say your name was?"

The lady harrumphed. "I didn't say because you never had the manners to ask." She straightened her narrow shoulders and raised her pointed chin. "I'm Agatha Bentley."

CHAPTER FOUR

My eyes widened. "You can't be Agatha Bentley. Agatha Bentley died. Her funeral was yesterday. You were there, remember?" The poor old lady had lost her mind. She had probably been one of Agatha's friends and was in some form of denial about her death. I felt bad for the old woman, but I really needed her to leave nonetheless. I had my own problems to deal with and the last thing I needed was to babysit some angry lady who thought she was my deceased boss.

"Of course, I was there," she snapped. "You really think I would miss my own funeral? These things only come around once in a lifetime, don't you know."

I squeezed my eyes shut and rubbed my eyelids with my fingertips. The poor woman was probably distraught and needed help. "I understand you must be upset, ma'am. It's never easy to lose a friend. Is there anywhere I can take you? Maybe I can call a cab for you or something?"

Exasperated, the woman raised her hands above her head and gave me the most curious of expressions. "My dear girl, I haven't lost anyone. What are you going on about? Maybe you are right? Maybe you're crazy after all."

Okay, that was it. I'd had enough. I marched up to her and reached out to place my hand on her shoulder so I could guide her out. But my hand fell through her as if she were nothing. I gasped and took a step back, my hand frozen in place. I blinked a few times and reached back toward her, her expression amused. She simply stood there, waiting as once again my fingers went right through her like she was air. I waved my hand back and forth and up and down, but still, nothing. My blood ran cold as I watched my hand pass right through her very body.

"Are you just about done?" she asked, frowning.

"This is impossible," I mouthed. *Inhale, count to three, exhale.*

"Oh, for goodness sake." The old woman threw her hands in the air. "You can practice Dr. Lee's breathing techniques all you want, girl, but it's not going to change anything."

I gaped at her. "You know Dr. Lee?" It was a stupid question to ask. Who cares if she knew who Dr. Lee was; we had bigger issues at hand. There was a strange woman in my newly inherited thrift shop who was claiming to be dead and somehow, by some trick of my imagination, didn't seem to be physically there. I took a few steps back from her and wrapped my arms tightly around my body, controlling my breath as I tried to make sense of things. "You're just a figment of my imagination. The stress has finally got to me. Talking cats and formless old women; absolute nonsense. All I need is a good night sleep, a hot bath, maybe a visit to a shrink, and then everything will be back to normal."

"Whatever you say, dearie." The old lady continued running her finger haphazardly along the surface of the counter. She looked bored and let out an extremely loud yawn.

I moved over to a large purple velvet chair in the corner and plunked myself down. I tucked my knees up and sunk back into the pillows, trying my best to relax. I watched the three cats. The tabby stretched out in the sunlight, disinterested in what was going on, but the ginger cat and the black one watched us closely. The old woman stared at me, but I tried not to look her in the eye, diverting my gaze in any direction but hers. "This is all just my imagination."

"That's fine, let's play this your way," the old lady said. "If this is your imagination, obviously it's trying to tell you something, don't you think?"

I nodded slowly, agreeing. "That makes sense. Okay,

what is my brain trying to tell me? What are you doing here? What do you want from me?"

The woman positively beamed and skipped toward me looking mischievous. "Now that, girlie, is the right question."

"Great, well, what is it?" I pressed. "Why am I imagining an old lady and three talking cats, huh?"

The cats perked up and sauntered over toward us, each taking a place near the chair as they looked up at me with their bright eyes. I did my best to ignore them and met the woman's gaze.

"First of all, you're not imagining things, that's plainly obvious." The woman crossed her arms and tapped her foot as she looked down at me, her eyes filled with judgment. "The reason you're here right now, is that I need you to do something for me. But first, I need you to believe that I'm not just a figment of your imagination."

I gaped at her, realizing how ridiculous it would seem to anyone who might walk by and look through the window: a crazy girl talking to an equally batty old woman in the middle of a cluttered thrift shop. Or just a broken girl talking to a figment of her own fractured imagination. I wasn't sure which scenario I preferred. "Fine. Go ahead. Convince me that I'm not imagining all this and that you're Agatha Bentley and your three talking cats are real. Good luck."

"Well. Your name is Priscilla Jones, you come from

Portland where you left your failed business and failed relationship behind." The woman raised her eyebrow at me, as if challenging me to deny her words. I merely grunted and allowed her to carry on. "You moved to Salem to live in my basement apartment—you don't want to, by the way, mine is much nicer—and to work for me in my thrift shop. We negotiated a three-month contract and you demanded an absolutely ridiculous pay rate of eighteen dollars an hour, but I'm only going to pay you thirteen."

I heaved a sigh. "Of course you know all that. Because I know all that and you're just a figment of my imagination. Tell me something I don't know."

The woman scrunched her wrinkled face as she pondered for a long moment. "Fine. How about this? My body was found here in the thrift shop after I choked, or apparently choked, on something. I'd been here for two days before anyone came to look for me. I was wearing this exact same outfit on the day of my death. I was found by a boy of the name Frankie, who often wears pants even tighter than those ridiculous ones you're wearing right now."

I brought out my phone as she spoke. I hadn't heard any of this before, but it could be just as easy for my brain to make up such a story. I bet myself $100 that if I searched the old woman's facts, nothing would come up. That would prove that this is all in my head and I was just losing my mind a little bit. Nothing a superfood smoothie and some meditation couldn't fix. Scrolling through the online news reports, my mouth dropped open. After furiously reading through a few websites and blogs that outlined the occurrences of Agatha's death, my skin grew cold. "It's true," I whispered.

"Of course, it's true, stupid girl. We're talking about my own death here. Or, at least, what I've managed to figure out about it," the old woman grumbled.

I frowned at my cell phone. "Maybe I read this somewhere, and I just don't remember."

Agatha proceeded to list out a number of other facts about herself that I would have no way of knowing, all of which I confirmed through quick internet searches. After about ten minutes of searching, there was no question that what she was saying was true. She wasn't a figment of my imagination at all. But how the hell could that be? I simply sat and stared at her. "So, you're what, a ghost?" I finally asked.

Agatha raised her hands above her head and shouted, "Hallelujah, the girl's not an idiot after all!"

I ran my hands through my hair nervously. "This is absurd. There is no such thing as ghosts. And absolutely no such thing as talking cats."

"Whatever you need to tell yourself so you can sleep at night, beautiful," the tabby cat purred.

"This just doesn't make sense," I whispered. "How can it? There must be some logical explanation for this. I've lost my mind, surely."

"The only thing you've lost is too much weight, skinny girl," Agatha snapped. She reached down and stroked the ginger cat's ear. "I hope she's not another disappointment, Muffin. We've had enough silly assistants to last us a lifetime, haven't we?"

"Your assistant?" I shook my head and was surprised something didn't rattle inside my aching skull. "What are you talking about? I can't assist you with anything, Agatha. You're dead." I swallowed hard, and decided to go upstairs, have a nice hot bath, get a proper night's sleep, and then book a session with the local therapist. "I don't think dead people really need assistants."

"Of course they do, you foolish girl. I need an assistant now more than ever." Agatha straightened herself and turned to look me square in the face. "I need you to solve my murder."

CHAPTER FIVE

"NOPE." AGATHA FOLLOWED ME THROUGH THE THRIFT store, but I refused to glance in her direction. "Nope, nope, nopety-nope."

"You can't nope me out of your life, girl. You signed a contract. You agreed to be my assistant." Agatha frowned at her hands. "And your first duty is to discover who murdered me so I can get my magic back and gain access to my powers."

I paused with my handle on the shop door. "Your magic?" I raised my eyebrows. "Your powers?" The ghost nodded and I scrunched my face up. "Yeah, we're done here." I lifted my hand. "Ghosts? Kinda, maybe. Talking cats? Stretching it. But magical powers?" I twisted my key in the lock and yanked the door open. "I'm out."

I let the door slam behind me as I pounded up the

stairs into the apartment, but when I slipped inside, Agatha was already waiting for me. I gritted my teeth as she followed me into the dining room and watched me haul my bags across the floor. "You know, you're not the only one who's disappointed with how this has turned out, young lady. You've got your panties all in a bunch because you're hard done by, but think how I must feel. I've signed all my worldly possessions over to a cowardly custard who lets slimy, good-for-nothing men control her life and then runs off like a lamb when they tell her they've had enough of her. Quitter."

Her accusation struck me like a blade and I spun to face her. "You know nothing about me!" I clenched my fists. "And I'm not running anywhere. I'm staying here and I'm turning your store into a juice bar, and you can haunt it all day and all night for all I care. I'm not a quitter."

"That's the spirit, Cilla." The ghost clapped her hands and called to the cats, "We'll make a fine witch out of her yet, boys."

"A witch?" I shouldered the door to the master bedroom open and flung my bags on the floor in an indignant pile. "Of course, how did I not see that coming? You're a witch. A ghost witch. And you were murdered and now I need to be your witch apprentice and uncover the truth of the dastardly crime, am I right?" The old woman nodded and I gave a snort of disbelief. "Yeah, that's not going to happen, lady. Sorry, the last train to crazy town is ready to leave the station, but I'm not getting on it. You and the cats are going to have to make that little trip alone."

Agatha narrowed her eyes at me. "You're lucky I don't have my powers, girlie. I'd be very tempted to teach you some manners, wouldn't I, boys?" In response to her question, the cats moved closer to Agatha's feet. The ginger cat, Muffin, purred affectionately at the ghost while the tabby cat prowled in a full circle around me, pausing briefly to run his eyes over my body before returning to Agatha. The black cat just glared. Agatha sniffed, watching me out of the corner of her eye. "Who would have thought a young lady could be so cruel to a poor, defenseless murder victim?"

I opened my mouth to tell the ghost she was the furthest thing from a defenseless victim I'd ever met, but my retort was cut short by the sound of rapping on the door downstairs. I glared at Agatha as the banging increased in volume. "This conversation isn't over," I insisted as I yanked the door of the apartment open and trampled down the narrow staircase. Through the frosted glass, I could make out two figures; one tall and narrow, the other short and rounded. I frowned and opened the door a crack. "Can I help you?"

"Welcome to the neighborhood, dear." I blinked as the aroma of spiced apples and warm pastry hit my nostrils and my eyes were immediately drawn to the golden crust on the apple pie being thrust through the gap between the door and my body. I took a step back as a plump figure pushed past me, pie first, and a pretty, round face beamed in my direction. "Dot Murphy, I own the bakery and coffee shop on the corner, Bewitching Bites."

Before I could respond, a second body slid through the half-opened doorway and stood beside Dot in the cramped base of the stairwell. The newcomer was as straight and sharp as her companion was warm and soft, and she caught my hand in a cool, firm handshake before I had even gathered my wits enough to greet the women. My gaze traveled from her hand all the way up her long slim arm until it settled on the steel gray eyes examining me from under a blunt white fringe. The woman was strikingly beautiful, despite the lines of age that wreathed her eyes and the corners of her lips. Or perhaps because of them; hers was a face that had lived a long life and emerged triumphant. Her mouth curved ever so slightly at the corners as she addressed me. "Bianca D'Arcy. Welcome to Salem."

Bianca D'Arcy. Dot Murphy. The names stirred a memory in the corners of my mind and I realized with a start that these were the two ladies Agatha had been hurling abuse at during her memorial service the day before. Bianca and Dot, the silver socialites of Salem, according to Tracy, the friendly vet. I released Bianca's hand and straightened my cardigan, the same one I'd been wearing the day before. "Hi, I'm Price Jones.

Thanks for the welcome; I really didn't expect anyone to visit. Thank you."

I reached for the apple pie, but Bianca nudged Dot, causing her to move onto the staircase before I could take it. Bianca smiled sweetly and gestured for Dot to continue walking. "Dot, go ahead and bring it upstairs. Put the coffee on, too, we won't have Price making the refreshments on her first morning as a Salem resident." My eyebrows peaked as I watched the two old ladies make their way toward the apartment as if it were their home instead of mine. Bianca glanced at me over her shoulder. "Close the door, dear. This old building is draughty enough to freeze my bones."

Mouth slack, I eased the door shut and followed the ladies up the stairs and into the apartment. By the time I reached the kitchen, the smell of coffee brewing filled the air. The ginger cat padded softly across the linoleum floor and stared up at Dot with bright eyes as she bustled around the room, pulling out fine bone china from the presses and cutting the apple pie. The tabby cat pounced onto the windowsill and eyed the steaming dish, licking his lips, but the black cat remained unmoving in the doorway, his blue eyes narrowed and his back arched. I felt my own spine stiffen in solidarity with the surly feline; this was far more neighborly intervention than I liked before I'd made my morning smoothie. Dot smiled at me and waved toward the table, Agatha's table—my table—as if it were her own. “Sit down, sweetheart. Coffee is nearly ready.”

Like an obedient child, I slid into one of the hard-backed chairs and rested my hands on the table. Bianca made her way around the living area slowly, her gray eyes examining every inch of the apartment like twin laser beams. I shifted awkwardly as she paused beside the half-empty tub of oatmeal in the sink with a curl of distaste on her narrow lips. “I dropped my breakfast this morning,” I said, by way of explanation for the concealed mess. “The cats startled me.”

“Those damn cats,” Bianca said. She rested her hip against the dresser and reached for the coffee Dot offered her—black, no sugar. “Disgusting creatures, I’ve no idea what Agatha saw in them. I told her a thousand times she needed to have them put down before they mauled her in her sleep. How could anyone trust cats that size? They’re bad enough when they’re tiny, but those three?” She jerked her head toward the living area where the cats had retreated, obviously as unimpressed with Bianca as she was with them, and spat, “They’re practically feral.”

Dot giggled nervously as she poured me a cup of coffee. I didn’t have the heart to tell her I only drank decaffeinated, but I held my hand out before she could fill the cup with fresh cream from the tub she had pulled from her large, straw purse. “No cream, thank you,” I insisted. “I’m vegan.”

"Vegan?" Dot echoed as she pushed the cup of black coffee in my direction. She glanced at Bianca. "Isn't that wonderful, Bianca? This young lady is vegan." Dot plonked herself into the chair at the far end of the table and spooned enough sugar to make a dentist cry into her coffee, topping it off with as much whipped cream as the cup could hold. "You must be so healthy, dear, all those vegetables and fruits. I wish I could eat a little more healthily, but I have such a sweet tooth." She gestured to the wedge of pie and cream on her plate with a rueful smile. "Occupational hazard."

"I understand, it smells delicious," I said. "If I could find good vegan pastries, I'd never stop eating them, either."

Dot's face fell as she stared at the pie. She lowered her fork onto the table. "Oh, my goodness. You can't eat the pie, there's butter in the crust. I'm so sorry." She pressed a plump hand to her cheek. "What kind of ninny brings a welcome gift that a person can't eat?"

"Don't be silly, it was a lovely gesture, you couldn't have known I was vegan," I reassured Dot.

"I should have brought something else as well. I should have checked first." Dot turned to Bianca with a frown. "I told you we should have sent a calling card first, but you wouldn't even leave it for a day. You had to get in here and poke your—"

"Dot." Bianca's voice had a warning edge as she interrupted her friend, and I dropped my gaze to stare into my cup. "You can bring Priscilla some vegan bread tomorrow, okay? Don't lose your head over pie."

I glanced at the taller woman in surprise. "You know my name?"

Dot's cheeks colored and she shoveled a heaped forkful of pie and cream into her mouth, chewing rapidly. Bianca didn't bat an eyelid. "It's a small neighborhood, dear; you'll find everyone on the street knows your name." She stepped away from the dresser and perched herself elegantly on the edge of a chair. "We're all quite curious about Agatha's mysterious beneficiary."

"You knew Agatha?" I asked, trying to avoid Bianca's probing stare. The black cat edged closer to the table and I wondered whether the ghost would make an appearance or whether she was sulking about the old ladies' presence. She hadn't seemed particularly fond of them at her funeral service.

"Yes. Agatha, Dot, and I go way back…" Dot cut another generous slice of pie for herself as Bianca began to speak, smothering it with cream and sprinkling extra sugar over the top. "We met the summer after high school. Dot's pop worked at Thomas Kay's woolen mill and he got us work there. Agatha had just moved to Salem to live with her aunt and she started on the line the same day as we did."

"She was smart," Dot said, her fork hovering halfway to her lips. The ghost of a smile passed over her pretty, plump face. "Not book smart like Bianca, but funny and clever. Even Josh Riggins was afraid to say anything in front of her in case she'd make a fool out of him." She glanced at Bianca. "He never called me butterball again after that first day when Agatha knocked him into the creek."

Bianca chuckled and the cats lifted their heads in surprise at the rich, warm swell of laughter. "Josh Riggins," she murmured. "I'd forgotten all about that little booger. She got him good."

"So you were friends since then? That's so nice, I don't really see any of my old friends anymore," I said. "Agatha was very lucky to have both of you in her life. You must have been a regular trio." My lips curved as I imagined the three old women sitting together, bickering and laughing.

Like a clam, Dot's lips sealed around her fork and she stared at the table. Bianca folded her arms and stiffened in the chair. "We had some good times, but life changed for all of us after that summer. We all left Salem to follow our paths and it's not all that long ago that we all ended up back in Salem again."

"And you reconnected then?" I prompted.

Dot reached for a third helping of pie, but Bianca blocked her hand and shot her a silent reprimand. The plump lady relinquished her hold on the pie and glanced at me with flushed cheeks. "Doll making," she said. I raised my brow. "We started a little doll making club, just the three of us. We used to meet at the café after hours. I didn't own the shop when we first started the club, I just worked in the kitchen, but Mr. Percy decided to sell up shop unexpectedly and I bought it from him then. It was Agatha who helped me come up with the name, you know? Bewitching Bites. Everybody loved it."

The catch in the old woman's voice tugged at my chest, and on instinct I leaned over and squeezed Dot's hand gently. "I'm sorry for your loss." I turned my head to address Bianca. "Both of you."

The tall woman stiffened in her chair and clasped her long fingers together tightly. "I'm afraid your sympathy is a little misplaced, Miss Jones. Agatha fell out with Dot and me,and we'd barely seen her in the months leading up to her death. In fact, she'd become quite the recluse, rarely left the building, and the people she did see, claimed she'd become somewhat…fanciful in her thoughts. Delusional, even." Bianca rested her elbows on the table and shrugged her shoulder. "I wouldn't be surprised if you found a load of old scribblings full of her crazy ideas lying around. Frankie, her assistant, said she was declaring him of all sorts of nonsense before they parted ways. Of course, after the way everything ended between those two, it's hard to know if he's just talking out of spite."

I eyed the cats warily out of the corner of my eye as Bianca finished speaking. Crazy Agatha falling out with her employees and pissing everybody off; sounded pretty accurate. And now I was talking to her ghost and hearing her cats speak. A knot tightened in my gut and I pushed my chair away from the table and started to clear the empty cups. "That's really sad, the poor lady," I said.

Dot sprang from her seat with surprising grace and started to pack everything away, clearly as anxious for the impromptu get-together to end as I was. Only Bianca remained seated. Her gray stare was trained on my face. "I'm sorry, dear. I didn't mean to upset you. I wasn't suggesting that her will could be overturned because of her mental state before her death." My hand froze halfway to the faucet over the sink and I met her eye. She smiled sweetly, the elegant curve of her lips doing nothing to soften the sharp predatory nature of her gaze. "I'm sure nobody thinks that for a second."

"I didn't ask for this." I turned my back to the sink, feeling the edge of the counter dig into my lower back. "I had no idea she was going to leave anything to me. I'm not some sort of social predator if that's what you think. Anyone who has a problem with Mrs. Bentley's will is more than welcome to take it up with her attorney."

Dot shook her head so hard that her white curls bounced around her cheeks. "Oh, no, that's not what we think at all. We don't want any of Agatha's money. I've got my shop and Bianca's the wealthiest woman in town, and even if we weren't, we wouldn't want a cent from Aggy's estate, right, Bee?"

"Of course," Bianca replied, stretching her legs as she stood from the table.

"Bianca was just trying to warn you, is all," Dot insisted. She grabbed hold of her purse and patted my arm gently. "There are always people who think they deserve more than they get in a neighborhood like this. Begrudgers, gossips, disgruntled employees—don't you pay any heed to them. If you need anything at all, you're always welcome at Bewitching Bites."

Dot swept out of the kitchen before I could say another word and the ginger cat padded softly after her, purring. I watched as she took a final glance around the room. She pressed her hand to her lips and closed her eyes for a moment, and then she was gone. Bianca nodded to me and I followed her to the door of the apartment, glancing around anxiously for any sign of the old witch. On the doorstep, she turned and faced me—eyes sharp, lips narrow—but she didn't say another word before she marched down the street after her friend. I noted that Bianca hadn't told me where to find her should I ever need her help.

CHAPTER SIX

By the time I hauled my tired bones back up the stairs to the apartment; Agatha had reappeared and was prowling around the hallway like a jaguar. She swiveled to glare at me as soon as I closed the apartment door. "Well, did you get any information from those old cows?"

"Information?" I burst through the bedroom door. I really needed some food. And a shower. No, I thought, a bath. I needed a long, hot bath.

The old woman stamped her ghostly feet in irritation. "Information about my murder. Did they do it? Well, not Dorothy, she doesn't have a bad bone in her roly-poly body, but Bianca? Ha, she'd put a knife in her own mother's back to make a quick buck."

"Oh, come on, Agatha. She'd not that bad," I said, Bianca's warning about the old lady's will slithering in the back of my mind. I screwed my face up. "Anyway, it's all irrelevant." I pulled my cell phone out of my pocket and flicked through the articles about Agatha's death for the second time that morning before flashing the screen at her face. "You choked on a grape, sorry. Murder solved, no witchcraft necessary." I raised my hands in a pleading gesture. "Now, could you please leave the room so I can get out of these filthy clothes and have a bath?"

"But it's not true." Agatha plonked herself down on the large bed and wrapped a weightless hand around the bars of the wrought iron frame. I slid my cell back into my pocket, taken aback by the ghost's sudden deflation. I unzipped my bags and pulled out a robe, a bath towel, and some fresh clothes and underwear. I hid the royal blue lacy lingerie set under my towel to prevent Agatha from ranting about young people and their tiny underwear, but the old woman didn't even glance in my direction as I shimmied out of my clothes and slipped into my robe. The tabby cat sat beside Agatha on the bed and grinned at me as I walked across the room, but the ginger cat hid his head under the comforter. The black cat appeared to have disappeared entirely. If getting undressed was all I had to do to make the cats vamoose, I decided I would happily take up naturalism. I was just about to close the door to the bathroom when the ghost spoke again. "I didn't just choke on a grape. That couldn't have been how it all ended. I wasn't done with life. I wasn't finished."

Despite myself, I softened, unable to ignore the depth of sadness in her voice. Sadness, or perhaps, regret. I pressed my palm against the doorframe. "You don't remember how you died?"

Like breaking a spell, the old woman was back to her usual, exasperated self. "Of course, I don't remember how I died, you nincompoop. Who the hell remembers their own death? That's why I need you, to work the memory spell and to avenge my murder."

I snapped the en-suite bathroom door shut in Agatha's face, but the old woman walked through it with a smug grin. Muttering under my breath, I twisted the taps and a flood of blessedly warm water gurgled from the spout and splashed into the huge porcelain tub. The bathtub's clawed feet were beautiful, as were the ceramic tiled floor and the handcrafted wall unit, but I suspected the oversized room would be draughty and cold once winter came again. I made a mental note to figure out how to work the heat in the building, grateful for whoever had ensured there was warm water for my bath. My head was full of the buzz of tiredness and a creeping awareness that talking to a ghost felt more natural than I wanted to admit. "Listen, Agatha, I'm not a witch. I'm a normal, suburban woman. There's nothing witchy or special about me; sorry to disappoint."

"What coven do you belong to?" Agatha narrowed her eyes. "Has somebody told you something about me? They've told you not to work with me."

"What? No," I said. "This is ridiculous. More ridiculous than the darn cats. I don't know how many times I need to tell you this, lady, but I'm not a witch."

Agatha waved her hand dismissively. "Of course you are, you scented your letter of application with lavender oil."

I rooted through the vanity and drawers, casting a glare over my shoulder. "I like essential oils. That doesn't make me a witch."

"I worked an overseer spell and I saw you drinking your green potions. I saw you trying to give one to that buffoon you were besotted with, too." Agatha crossed her arms and raised one eyebrow. "Spelled love never ends well, any witch worth her salt knows that much."

I snatched a bottle of bubble bath from a drawer and emptied it into the water. "Vegan smoothies." I snapped the drawer closed. "Not potions, smoothies. Because I'm a businesswoman, not a witch."

"Oh, for goodness sake, enough with this charade already. You think I don't recognize a witch when I see one?" Agatha threw her hands in the air. "Fiddlesticks and pork pies, next you'll be trying to tell me that boyfriend of yours doesn't have a teeny-tiny piece of equipment."

The tabby cat poked his head through the cat flap in

the bathroom door and his whiskers twitched as he glanced from me to his ghostly owner.

"Ex-boyfriend," I snapped, instinctively, narrowing my eyes. "And how would you know about my ex-boyfriend's… anything? Were you spying on him with your spell, too?"

"Absolutely not." Agatha held a hand to her chest as if the accusation offended her. "But if you insist on sniveling over your cell-phone thingy at night and flicking through pictures of him with his pathetic little—"

"Stop!" I clapped my hands over my ears and glared at the door. "Stop, stop, stop. Let me have my bath in peace, please." I tipped my head at the tabby cat perched lazily on the side of the bath. "And take that hairball with you."

Agatha tutted. "Don't call him a hairball, Pussy is a beautiful cat."

"Pussy?" I almost choked on the name. "You called a male cat Pussy?"

"Don't have such a filthy mind, child," Agatha drawled, but I could tell from the gleam in her eye and the twist of her lips that the humor wasn't lost on her.

The tabby cat arched his back and stretched his paws before pouncing onto the floor with a toss of his head. "Don't be like that, sweetheart. You're just feeling a little tense. Maybe a little time with a man who's packing more than a shrimp-sized—"

I grabbed the empty bottle of bubble bath and flung it as hard as I could. It sailed through Agatha's stomach and smacked off the wall above Pussy's head. "Get out, you psychopaths. Please." Agatha opened her mouth, but I cut her off. "No! Get out, get out, get out!"

With a roll of her eyes, Agatha vanished, leaving me alone with the smarmiest looking cat on the face of the earth. I waved a hairbrush threateningly and glared at him. Pussy stretched once more before he sauntered away. He looked over his shoulder as he approached the cat flap and blinked with one eye. "Have a nice bath, sweetheart. If you discover you have an…itch you want licked—"

The hairbrush bounced off the door as his tail disappeared.

CHAPTER SEVEN

"SLEAZY LITTLE FUR BAG," I MUTTERED AS I DIPPED MY toe into the bubble-filled bath. "Ouch." I recoiled from the scalding heat of the water and glared at the door. "Great, made me run my water too hot as well."

Grumbling, I made my way back to the bedroom to unpack my stuff while I waited for the bath to cool a little. I emptied my bags and placed my folded clothing into the dresser drawers in the airy bedroom. A bedroom, I suddenly realized, that had probably belonged to Agatha only days before. I stared at my belongings in the old woman's drawers and wondered what I was doing. Why was I unpacking? I wasn't sure if I was going to stay in the house with its cats and its ghostly witch. Hell, I wasn't sure if I was going to stay in Salem. I closed the drawer with a shove. "No sense making any hasty decisions, Price."

I grimaced at my reflection in the dresser mirror and made my way through the room. The décor screamed old woman, but with a few tweaks it wouldn't be that bad at all. Vintage chic was all the rage these days and something about it appealed to my inner old lady. Reminded me of a time before cell phones and social media and constant accessibility—a cell phone that buzzed with endless messages and calls from people who didn't really care if I lived or died.

There was a large window overlooking the back lane, which perhaps wasn't the most peaceful of views, but somebody had painted the back wall with bright splashes of color and hung flower baskets of artificial flowers amongst the fairy lights strung along the crumbling brick. I smiled, imaging Agatha and her old friends eating bologna sandwiches and drinking tea in the lane on warm summer evenings. "What a strange little place."

I plucked my jacket from the floor and hung it on the back of the door, emptying my keys from the pocket. I opened the drawer of the bedside table to tuck them in for safekeeping, and sitting in the drawer was a small diary, a thin layer of dust covering the front cover. I carefully picked it up and blew off the dust, revealing the name *Aggy* on the front. I couldn't help but cast a guilty look over my shoulder as I flipped open the front page. It wasn't any of my business going through someone else's diary, but the old woman was dead, so what harm could it do, right? And she'd snooped into my life with her spell, watching me try to win Gerard back, spying on my photos of— "Nosey little busybody."

I clutched the diary between my stiff fingers and marched back into the en-suite, tossing my robe onto the floor in a disgruntled heap. Still gripping Agatha's diary, I dipped my foot into the water. It was hot but bearable, and I slowly submerged my feet, followed by the rest of my body, inch by inch. The water against my skin felt invigorating, and I let out a soft sigh as I sunk down to my neck and floated in the massive tub. The surface was coated with bubbles, and the scents of lavender and citrus filled my nose. I closed my eyes and relaxed, relishing in the therapeutic benefits of the hot tub. Peace at last. Time to reconnect with Dr. Lee and find my Zen. *I'm a leaf, floating on a gentle current—*

"What's she doing?"

Clenching my teeth, I turned to see the three cats standing beside the bathroom door, cat flap swinging. The large black cat jumped up to the toilet seat and then onto the cistern, watching me from a safe distance with narrowed eyes the color of blue glass. The ginger cat sprawled in the middle of the floor and stretched out while the cheeky tabby, Pussy, sauntered around the tub, as if unsettled in the steamy room.

"What are you doing here?" I asked them. I should have locked the cat flap. If cat flaps could even be locked. Who installed a cat flap in a bathroom, anyway? In the event that I did stay, I mused, I'd have to seriously weigh the benefits of keeping the creepy fur balls or giving them away, perhaps to a neighbor or shelter. I was allergic, after all. My lips twitched up at the thought.

"She acts like she wants us to leave, but she's smiling. Women are so confusing." The ginger cat's voice was softer than the tabby cat's, less refined. I frowned at the cat's green eyes. Something about the bright stare reminded me of Gerard's best friend from grad school, a former quarterback and superstar-turned-business-major. He'd asked me on a date once, before Gerard and I got serious. He'd told me I could do better than Gerard. Guess I should have listened. The ginger rolled into a crouch. "Guys, she's staring at me. Why's she staring at me?"

Before I could answer him, a deep, gravelly voice filled the room. "She's not deaf, Muffin." The ginger cat's face swiveled in the black cat's direction and then back toward me, before he covered his eyes with a soft paw. The black cat's chuckle was so low it was almost a growl.

Pussy padded across the floor and rolled onto his back beside the ginger cat. "Fluffy's right, Muffin. She's not like the other people on the street, kid. Price is the new Agatha."

"I'm not the new Agatha," I snapped, glaring over at the tabby cat.

Pussy's mouth stretched wide and pointed teeth flashed at me. "Sure you're not, princess. You just let all that anger out." His eyes glinted in the sunlight. "Agatha always liked to talk things out in the tub, too."

I suppressed a scream of frustration and crossed my arms under the bubbles, turning my head away from Pussy and his infuriating grin. What the hell was I doing talking to a cat? Letting a cat get under my skin? A cat. I closed my eyes and forced myself to breathe deeply, but I had a hard time relaxing as the thoughts of the strange old woman's words ran through my head. I had the hardest time convincing myself that she was real, but at the same time, how could she have known those things that I had no way of knowing myself? Could my brain work like that? Maybe I'd imagined her walking through the wall, and perhaps she was a real person that had simply followed me home from the park. But no, that couldn't be right. My hand had gone right through her. I'd seen it. There was no way in hell I could be that crazy. Could I?

"She doesn't look like she's all that relaxed," Muffin's voice said from the side of the tub.

I jumped, splashing water over the side of the bathtub and onto the floor. This was simply getting out of hand. "Stop talking! You're a cat. I know you're not real. It is all my head."

"Give her a break, guys." The black cat's slow, smooth voice slid across the room. "She didn't know about any of this stuff—witches, spells, ghosts. She needs time to adjust."

I raised my hands to my ears and sunk deeper into the tub. "La, la, la."

Pussy prowled along the edge of the tub and pressed his nose closer to my face. "I don't know, Fluffy, she mightn't be able to handle it. She's got a bag in the other room that *says* 'Peace, Love, and Yogalates.' What kind of crap is that?"

"She's a hippie, that's for sure," Fluffy said.

My eyes flew open at his words. I turned to face the black cat and glared at him. "Who are you calling a hippie?"

"You," the black cat replied. "Come on, I bet you have hemp smoothies for breakfast and avocado toast for brunch, am I right?"

I stared at him for a long moment, contemplating whether I was going to play into the whole crazy thing and argue with the stupid, blue-eyed cat. I finally decided I had already reached the maximum threshold of crazy; I might as well give in to my failing brain. "You don't have breakfast and brunch on the same day, idiot." I flashed him a smug grin, certain that would shut him up, but I swear the cat rolled his eyes at me. "Besides," I added. "Hemp smoothies are extremely nutritious and avocados are underrated."

The black cat feigned a cough. "Hipster."

"Fleabag," I retorted. The black cat chuckled in response and I felt my lips curve, despite myself. I shook my head and reached for the old lady's diary, refusing to acknowledge the fact that I'd enjoyed the little exchange. I was not the kind of woman who exchanged banter with a cat. I began flipping through the pages of the journal, but I couldn't understand a word of it. Magic and spells? Hardly. The book was nothing but utter jibberish. I came to page with a pretty pencil drawing of a cat and I shifted to examine it more closely, my interest peaking. Tucking my legs up toward me, I sat up straight and read it aloud to hear the strange sounds of the unfamiliar language. *"Redire ad se verum est, quod magica de oppanso corporis tui concelavi."*

I felt a strange rush of energy flow through me as I spoke the words aloud, and I swear, the room shimmered around me. A bright flash of light filled the air and suddenly, in place of the cats, stood three extremely naked men.

CHAPTER EIGHT

"WHAT THE HELL!" I SHRIEKED. I THREW THE JOURNAL across the room and my arms and legs splashed wildly as I tried to conceal my body, sliding awkwardly under the water and gasping for breath. I threw my body halfway over the edge of the bathtub, swearing as I grabbed my robe, wrapped it around myself, and headed for the door. I'd barely taken a step when my foot slipped on the tiles and I collided with a hard, muscular body. I reached out to steady myself and my hand grabbed a piece of anatomy so impressively huge that I immediately let go in shock, catapulting myself back into the cold bathwater. "Holy sh—"

"Swearing is most unbecoming for a lady your age." With a loud pop the old lady appeared in the bathroom, perched high on the sink with her short, skinny legs dangling below.

My voice raised an octave. “What in damnation is going on here?” It was the final straw, the one that broke the metaphorical camel’s back; I had lost it. Categorically, undeniably, call the doctors, lost it. Reality was no longer the realm I existed in. There was no way in hell that I could truly be sitting soaked in the bathtub surrounded by three naked men and a crazy old lady ghost. It simply wasn’t happening. There was no way this could be happening to me.

“Well, that was unexpected,” a soft voice said. I gaped at the man with dark auburn hair and leaf-green eyes through a haze of disbelief. He was tall and fair skinned with shoulders so broad they could fill a door. My eyes traveled down his toned body to narrowed hips and defined abdominal muscles. Instinctively my gaze flickered lower and the man attempted to cover himself with his large hands. I twisted my head, trying to focus anywhere but on what I’d just seen. He wasn’t the man I’d grabbed, but still... I chanced a peek at his face and saw his cheeks were as flushed as I was certain my own were.

A towel landed on the redhead's shoulder. “Here, man, cover it up in front of the lady.” I blinked at the sound of the low, gravelly voice coming from a dark-haired man with olive skin and tousled black hair. He didn’t meet my eye as he wrapped a towel around his waist, but from the brief glance I got before the fabric concealed his form, there was no denying he was the man I'd collided with before I fell back into the bathtub. I ran my hand over my forehead. I needed to get out of this room. It was too damn hot.

"I don't need a towel, Fluffy. I'm perfectly comfortable in this skin." I could barely bring myself to face the third man as he lounged against the door. His long body was slender, lean, and tanned all over as if he'd spent hours lying under the warm sun. I studiously avoided looking below his waist, aware he was scrutinizing every flick of my gaze. Out of the corner of my eye, I saw his smile widen and the dimple in his chin deepen. His white blonde hair looked like he spent every moment surfing on the West Coast, but I'd spent enough time around Gerard's friends to know his unkempt 'do probably cost more than my juice bar had made on its best week. Eyebrows curved above sparkling hazel eyes. "Don't be shy, sweetheart, we're all friends here. Although, you still haven't made us any breakfast…"

No. No, no, no. I didn't believe it. It couldn't be happening. Sure, the voices were the same, but there had to be an explanation. It was all a set-up. I was being filmed. I gripped my robe tighter around my chest and shouted, "Punked! You got me, people. You got me, good."

The man with the auburn hair frowned and took a step forward. "Is she okay, guys? She doesn't look okay."

Agatha crossed her arms and swung her legs. "Oh, she's all right; it just seems the snoopy little witch found my spell book."

"Spellbook?" I mouthed slowly, staring at the leather-bound journal on the floor. We'd deal with the pot-kettle-blackness of her accusing me of being the snoop later. First, spells; later, indignant rage, I decided.

"Yes, my spell book, girlie. And now look what you've done." Agatha waved a finger at the three men. "Didn't anyone teach you not to meddle in another witch's business?"

"I am not a witch." My voice was a shadow of its former self.

"Definitely a witch," the dark, brooding man with the big…blue eyes said. "You have far too many weird herbs and stuff in your bag to not be a witch."

"They're just herbs," I snapped.

"Witch herbs," the blond man added. He let out a wolf-whistle and winked at the other two men. "Can I just say, you're looking good there, Muffin, Fluffy…"

"Shut it, Pussy," the dark-haired man snapped. From the way he squared his ink-covered shoulders, I guessed he wasn't the kind of guy you messed with. He picked up the last towel from the floor and flung it at the blond man. "Put it on."

"Oh, cut it out, all three of you," Agatha barked as the blond covered himself with a towel. The ghost jumped from her perch on the sink and sprang across the bathroom to pick up the diary from the floor. I raised a brow in surprise. I couldn't feel her, but she could move objects. Interesting. "And you!" The ghost pointed a thin finger in my direction. "My diary is none of your business, do you hear me? A witch's spells are private. Keep your paws to yourself before you ruin any more of my work. How the hell am I supposed to fix these three when I don't have any access to my magic?"

"Fix these three?" I repeated. I sounded like a babbling idiot, repeating everything Agatha said.

"You okay there, Priscilla? Do you need anything? You look like you're about to pass out or something. You're really pale." The auburn-haired man looked concerned as he leaned against the far wall of the bathroom.

"Price," I corrected. I spread my fingers wide, palms upturned. "And yes, I do need something. I need there not to be half-naked men in my bathroom. Why are you all half-naked?"

The dark-haired man lifted his chin. "You expected us to have some magical cat clothes? Fur that transforms into jeans and a shirt?"

"Besides, we're not the only ones half-naked, here," the blond man teased, running a slow gaze over my bare legs and the soaked robe clinging to my skin.

Agatha made a heaving noise. "Oh, for goodness sake, stop prattling and flirting, all of you. It's nauseating." She flicked a hand toward the men.

"There's a reason I turned you into cats in the first place; pets are so much more pleasant than people."

I stared at the ghost. "You turned—"

"Us into cats?" The dark-haired man finished. His blue eyes flashed as he turned to the other two men. "What the hell? Did you two know this?"

The auburn-haired man drew his brows together as if he was trying to catch an elusive memory. "No…" He shook his head. "I don't know. Maybe?"

"Of course, you didn't know, that's the nature of the curse. A familiar never remembers its former existence." Agatha glowered at me. "Unless some other magic interferes with the spell."

I glared at the ghost. "Oh, please, you turned these men into cats, but you want to make me out to be the bad guy? I don't think so, ghost-witch."

Agatha tossed her head. "Pooh, pooh. How do you know they didn't deserve it? They could be mass murders for all you know." At my tentative glance to my right, she added, "or rapists."

I eyed the men as they glared at the ghost. What a shame to waste such beauty on villains. "And were they?" I asked.

The ghost shrugged. "How should I know? I'm dead." The three men took a step closer to the witch, their stares as sharp as mine. We waited for her to elaborate. Agatha sighed as if she was exhausted by our collective ignorance. "I'm a dead witch; I'm bound by the Law of the Dead. I can't access my powers or recall the details of my most powerful spells until I've resolved my unfinished business." She wagged a finger at the men. "I have no recollection why I chose such distracting creatures to be my pets." The ghost fixed her glare on me. "And now you've stuck your beak into the spell, who knows what way the magic will react."

"How can we fix this stupid Law of the Dead business?" I asked, trying not to stare at the three men. "I mean, we need to figure out if these guys deserve to get back to their real lives or if they're dangerous criminals that should be behind bars." I glanced in their direction. "No offense."

"None taken," the dark-haired man growled.

The red-haired man raised one large hand. "I actually do take some offense at that. I'd rather if we didn't assume I'm a rapist or murderer, if that's cool?"

Agatha ignored both men and stepped close enough to me that I noticed the delicate blue of her eyes for the first time. Baby blue. "There's only one way to appease the law, Priscilla." I didn't bother to correct her. "Resolve my unfinished business; find my murderer."

CHAPTER NINE

"Agatha, you weren't murdered." The ghost stared down her nose at me with a disapproving frown and I held my hands up. "I'm sorry, I really am, and I'm no expert in criminal forensics, but a grape isn't a murder weapon." The blond man snorted and I gave him a sharp glance. "Where the hell were you guys when she died anyway? Chasing mice?"

From the look on the men's faces, I was pretty certain I'd hit a nerve. The dark-haired man crossed his strong, tattooed arms. "We were out. By the time we got back, she was…gone." Something about the weight in his eyes sucked the anger from my bones and I dropped his stare.

Ding-dong.

The echo of the doorbell rang through the house. Grateful for the distraction, I jumped from the tub, dripping wet, and reached for a towel to find there were none left. The blond man dropped his hand to his waist and made to loosen his towel, and I slapped my hands over my eyes. “No! No more nakedness, please.”

“I don’t know, I quite enjoyed the nakedness when you were getting changed earlier,” the blond drawled. I could practically see his grin despite my closed eyes.

The sound of a drawer opening and closing was followed by something soft being shoved against my hands. “Here.” I recognized the dark-haired man’s deep tones. “We’ll all turn around so you can put it on.”

I lowered my hands to find all three men with their backs turned to me and the blond man grumbling loudly about gender equality and roaming female eyes. I couldn’t help but smirk as I peeled off my soaking wet robe and tried to rub myself off with a hand towel. Three pairs of taut buttocks winked at me from beneath thin cotton towels.

“Ahem.” Agatha nodded pointedly toward the door as the sound of the doorbell rang out again. I pulled on the frilly pink robe and secured it as tightly as it could. On me, Agatha’s robe only reached mid-thigh and gaped at the chest in a way that would have been indecent on somebody with a more generous bust.

I bolted out of the room and down the stairs toward the front door before the three men had a chance to turn around again.

Opening the door a crack, I poked my head through

to see who was there. A short, elderly man I vaguely recognized from the funeral stood on the front step, looking rather nervous. "Miss Priscilla Jones?"

I nodded, glancing back quickly into the entryway behind me. To my dismay, the three cat-men and the old crazy lady stood behind me, eagerly peering over me to see who was at the door. I glared at them and turned back to the short man. I stopped halfway through the doorway, pulling it tight behind me so the poor guy at the doorstep couldn't see the motley crew behind me.

"Price," I forced a smile as I replied to him. "You can call me Price. What can I do for you?"

I could hear the three guys and the old lady squabbling on the other side of the door. I waved my right hand slightly in an attempt to shush them, but they simply raised their voices and spoke louder. Eager to make the stranger on the doorstep go away, I smiled at him and nodded encouragingly, hoping he'd hurry with whatever the heck it was he wanted. The last thing I needed was for someone else to witness the disaster going on inside. Or worse still, have someone confirm my biggest fear that all this was just a figment of my imagination and I was indeed going crazy.

"Well, Miss Jones," the man said. He fumbled in his jacket pocket and pulled out a crisp cotton handkerchief which he twisted nervously as he spoke. "Price, I mean. Price. I work at a small law firm just down the road. I was the one who managed Mrs. Bentley's affairs and she was... well, she was kind to me. And she was very happy when she called me and asked me to come help put her affairs in order a few weeks ago. She was excited to work with you, and she told me that you didn't know anything about the estate being in your name. That she wasn't going to tell you anything. That it was what she wanted; she was a very strong-minded woman, you know, very capable."

"I see," I said slowly, uncertain where on earth the conversation was going.

The man swallowed hard. "Well, I just wanted to let you know before you heard from another source; some new evidence came to light following the pathology report and Mrs. Bentley's death is being investigated as suspicious. And, well, with you arriving so suddenly and inheriting everything so unexpectedly…" My mouth fell open a little as the cogs in my brain began to turn. The man gave me a tight smile. "I'm very sorry, Miss Jones. I just wanted to warn you before anything happens, and to let you know I'm here if you need any legal support. I owe it to Mrs. Bentley."

Before he could add anything else, I offered a forced handshake, thanked him, and hurried back inside. The entryway was deserted, the cats and their owner, their real owner, had obviously decided the old man wasn't worth eavesdropping on. I peered through the peephole and watched the small, balding man as he stood on the doorstep for a moment before plodding away. I had never even asked his name. As soon as he was gone, I turned on my heels and ran back up the stairs, yelling for Agatha.

I stormed into the bedroom and the ghost appeared beside the window. "I told you I was murdered." Agatha's face was alive with smug triumph. "Now do you believe me?"

I rubbed my eyes with the palms of my hands and sank down onto the edge of the bed. "You did tell me." I glanced up at her and chewed on my bottom lip for a moment. "I'm sorry, Agatha. That I didn't believe you, and that, well, you know."

"That I was murdered in cold blood?" The ghost asked. "That I was savagely ripped to shreds in the prime of my life?" I drew my brows low and pressed my lips together. She was pushing it a bit with the 'prime of her life' nonsense. She was no spring chicken.

A shadow fell on the wooden floorboards as three figures crowded into the room. The blond guy cocked his head and made a face. "Come on, Aggy, the murder weapon was a grape and you're at least a hundred. It's uncool, but it's hardly Jack the Ripper standard."

The red-haired man knocked his friend halfway across the room with a nudge of his broad shoulders. "She was murdered, Pussy. It's not a joke." He turned gentle green eyes on the elderly ghost. "Are you okay, Ag? I mean, I know you thought somebody had… Jeez. This sucks."

The dark-haired man leaned his weight against the door frame and crossed his arms over his still bare chest. I eyed the towel slung distractingly low on his hips and wondered were there any clothes in the store that would fit the three men. I had enough on my plate without the added complication of damp, ludicrously enticing bodies lounging on all sides. The man inclined his head in my direction. "And hipster here is in prime position to take the fall for a crime she didn't commit. It's bullcrap."

The other men nodded, even Pussy looked somber as he pushed a lock of blond hair out of his hazel eyes. Agatha tipped her head in agreement. "It is. Total poppycock." Her lips twisted into a grin as she turned in my direction. "It does have one upside, though."

I raised my eyebrows and stared at the ghost, waiting for her to reveal the silver lining to the poop sandwich I'd been handed. She schooled her mouth into what I gathered was her best attempt at a winning smile. "Now, you've got no choice but to help find my murderer, and quick-smart, before—"

"Before I get blamed for your murder," I muttered.

She was right, damn it. Things just got personal.

CHAPTER TEN

An overwhelming exhaustion flooded through my bones as I sank into an armchair in the living room. I folded my hands in my lap and stared straight ahead, seeing nothing.

"She's doing that thing again where she doesn't speak and makes a face like a robot," a voice I recognized as belonging to the red-haired man whispered.

I glanced up in time to catch the man with dark hair and tattooed skin nudging his friend. "Not helping, man."

The blond guy, Pussy, leaned casually against the doorframe, striking his trademark pose as if he were pulled straight from Calvin Klein magazine. "Is she even still alive? Someone should poke her. I volunteer—"

"Touch me and you lose a hand," I snapped. "Or a paw, whatever." I pushed myself up off the chair and began pacing the room. "I'm trying to think, and I can't do that with you guys distracting me."

"Well that's just something you have to get used to," the blond man drawled. "We're very distracting."

I eyed his slow grin and my lips twisted upward of their own accord, but they quickly thinned as thoughts of my current predicament crowded my mind again. I turned toward the three men, wondering where the ghost had disappeared to; she certainly knew how to pick her moments. "What am I going to do? A murder suspect? It's ridiculous. Yesterday I was in Portland clearing my stuff out of the pool house…" I let my words trail off, aware of the way the men were avoiding my eye. Clearly, they hadn't missed Agatha's jibes about my sad, pathetic life back home. Things were really bad when men who'd been furry house pets an hour ago were shooting you pitying glances. I lifted my jaw and channeled my inner Dr. Lee. "What I mean is, I only just arrived in Salem, so how could anybody think I had something to do with Agatha's death?"

The room fell silent for a long moment before the gravelly voice of the dark-haired man filled the room. "Agatha changed her will, with no warning or explanation, and died under suspicious circumstances only days later. And now, here you are; inheriting everything she owns, living in her home when you had nowhere else to go. It wouldn't take Sherlock Holmes to figure you're worth investigating."

"Are you suggesting I had something to do with Agatha's death?" I shot him a murderous glare. "You know that's nonsense, I didn't even recognize her ghost."

The slightest hint of pink colored the tattooed man's cheeks and his scowl intensified. "I'm just telling you what the cops are probably thinking. Nobody can help you if you're going to act like a delusional idiot."

"He's right." The blond guy nodded. "Fluffy might be a bad-tempered jerk with no sense of fun or adventure." The dark-haired man glared at him. "But he's not stupid. The cops are going to be all over your cute butt."

I pursed my lips. "Thanks for that, Pussy."

The blond smiled like I'd paid him a compliment. "You're welcome, doll. Anytime."

I released a loud groan in his direction. "I was being sarcastic, you idiot."

"I know." His grin widened, white teeth gleaming.

I reached for the pillow behind me and threw it at him, narrowly missing his head and accidentally knocking over a small vase on the end table across the room. It fell to the ground and shattered, causing my heart to race even faster as my deep-rooted politeness clicked into gear.

"Oh, my goodness, I'm so sorry," I called to nobody

in particular. I scrambled across the floor on my hands and knees to clean up the mess I had made, but the dark-haired man blocked my path with hands that were surprisingly gentle and directed me back to the chair before collecting the broken pieces of china in a small cardboard box. My head fell back onto the cushioned velvet chair, and I pressed the palms of my hands into my closed eyelids. "What am I going to do?"

The red-haired man pushed himself up off the couch and crossed the room with concern etched into the smooth contours of his face. While the blond man was arrogantly handsome and the tattooed guy had an undeniable aura of brooding sexiness, the redhead was beautiful in a way I had rarely seen before. His pale skin was rich and creamy, and his green eyes, framed with thick, dark lashes, seemed to project his every thought and feeling. As he kneeled next to me and placed a large, graceful hand on my leg, empathy oozed from every inch of his body in a surge of hot intensity. "It's going to be okay, Price. We'll figure this out, right?" He looked at the other two men for reassurance and they both nodded. He turned and stared into my eyes again. "We just need to make sense of what's going on here." He glanced down at his half-naked body and the skimpy towel wrapped around his waist as if suddenly aware that he had very recently been a cat. His brow furrowed. "There has to be a logical explanation, and we can solve this together. I know we can."

His optimism was endearing, but I knew for a fact that we were totally screwed. Well, I was. They weren't, necessarily. Unless you count the whole magically turning into cats thing. I closed my eyes for a moment and ran my hand through my hair. Who was I kidding? We were all well and truly, royally screwed. "A logical explanation," I echoed. "You're right, I just need to ask the right questions. Does anyone happen to know what those would be?" I opened my eyes and looked around the room hopefully, but was simply met with blank stares. My fingers tapped the velvet upholstery as I sat there impatiently, my mind spinning.

Agatha came floating into the room, her eyes glazed over as she hummed a tune to herself. She came halfway into the space before realizing we were there and snapped out of her daze. "What are you all doing here?" She eyed the red-haired man's hand, still resting gently on my knee. "Muffin, why are you mauling my assistant."

With glowing cheeks and flustered excuses the man retreated to the other side of the room. Ignoring the ache in the base of my stomach as I was left alone again, I pulled my legs up so I was sitting cross-legged in the chair. "Agatha, you're exactly the person we need to talk to."

The ghost raised her eyebrows but settled her feet on the ground. "I guess I have nowhere else to be."

I twisted the ragged ends of my hair as I thought

carefully. "Why did you leave this place in my name? Why did you leave me everything you owned, even your..." My eyes darted to where the men stood for a moment, examining in the bare skin and the defined muscles through the curtain of my eyelashes. "Pets?"

Agatha stood before me, her diminutive height bringing her head to nearly the height of my own as I sat on the chair. She stepped closer to me as she pondered the answer, and I noticed the heavy wrinkles that lined her face. She was a soft-looking woman, delicate in a way, but I didn't let that fool me or interfere with my knowledge of how feisty she could be. She finally shrugged at me and turned a critical eye on the cushion lying against the wall.

"Is that all I'm going to get? A shrug?" I asked, hoping she didn't notice the missing vase before she'd given me some answers. "Come on, Agatha, I think you owe me more than that."

"I don't owe you anything, you selfish little cream puff," Agatha snapped right back at me, her nostrils flaring. "I gave you my house and my thrift shop, what more do you bloody want? Apart from my unwavering good looks, perhaps."

We both stared at each other for a long moment before I finally broke the silence. "Look, I'm grateful you left these things to me, I really am. But I'm confused. We've never met each other, and I only just replied to your ad a week or so ago. Why on earth would you ever leave all your worldly possessions to someone you didn't know? It seems completely ludicrous, doesn't it?" Seeing her features twist, I softened my tone. "I'm sorry, I don't mean to upset you. I'm just trying to understand."

"Maybe," Agatha started, pausing to draw her eyebrows close together. "Maybe I felt sorry for you? When I saw you living in that little shack behind that buffoon's fancy-pants mansion, well, I wouldn't wish that groveling, pathetic life on my worst enemy. Not even on Dorothy Murphy or Bianca D'Arcy." I opened my mouth to defend myself, but before I could gather some fighting spirit, the old woman's face crumpled. "But the truth is, Priscilla, I simply don't know the answer. These past few days, I've been trying to think and remember and understand, but I can't. It's as if that part of my brain has been blocked. There's just nothing there."

CHAPTER ELEVEN

"You don't remember anything about why you left the store and this building to Price, Aggy?" Bright blue eyes narrowed on the old woman floating in the middle of the living room as Fluffy folded his tattooed arms, muscles bulging under his inked skin. "You think it's some sort of magic blocking your memory? Like whatever is stopping you from remembering what happened to us, that 'Law of the Dead' bullshit?"

"Yes, perhaps, the law is blocking me from remembering anything tied magically to my unfinished business in this world," Agatha mused. Her face scrunched in concentration, her body vibrating. When she finally opened her mouth and her voice came out in a frustrated squeak. "Maybe."

Without another glance in my direction, the old witch floated across the room and out the far door.

"Agatha, wait," I called after her. She stalled and turned, her expression completely blank as she looked back at me. "Is there anything else you can think of that might help me clear my name? Surely, you must have some idea of who could've been behind your death?"

"I told you, I have no memory of my murder. That's the nature of passing from life to death, it's always this way." Agatha frowned and chewed her lower lip before shaking her head slowly from side to side. "And I have no idea why anyone would wish me harm. I was very well-liked in the community. Quite popular, actually. No one had any reason to dislike me; I was quite simply delightful."

I caught raised brows and an amused glance passing between the three men at her last words, and I suppressed a grin. "I can imagine you were, Agatha. You're a very likable woman." I could barely say it with a straight face. "So, you seem to have some sort of memory blockage or absence of any sort of knowledge of the events surrounding your death? Is that right?"

Agatha nodded and returned to the center of the room, her eyes dimming as her shoulders slumped. "But I fear it goes far deeper than that, dearie. I can't seem to remember much of anything, if I'm being perfectly honest. Perhaps, I left a lot of unfinished business behind."

I bit my lower lip before replying, a deep sadness filling me. "I'm sorry." It also made things rather more difficult for me, to be perfectly honest, but I wasn't going to ruin her moment. Without any memory of her past life or the events leading to her death, I had no way of getting any closer to figuring out who was actually behind it all.

"Seems to me, you'll have to stick around and do some sleuthing on your own, Miss Pricetag," the blond man said with a sly grin.

I noticed he mentioned me, not us. "Don't call me that, Pussy," I snapped. I folded my arms over my chest, ignoring the way my body responded to his slow grin. "I suppose you're full of ingenious suggestions, right?"

He shrugged and met my gaze, full lips curved upward and hazel eyes fixed on my face. "Dot and Bianca had plenty to say earlier, they might be able to lead you in the right direction."

"You think it was worth paying attention to?" The dark-haired man asked, brushing a stray dark lock out of his piercing blue stare. His expression darkened. "I suppose it did end badly between Aggy and him, not exactly an amicable parting of ways."

The red-head leaned his weight against the door frame. "Sucks, doesn't it? He was the best. Remember that mackerel fried in butter and garlic he used to make us? And he cleaned up the store so nicely."

"Frankie," I exclaimed, suddenly catching up with the men's shared train of thought. "Agatha's old assistant. Bianca had mentioned that he was bad mouthing Agatha all over town since she'd fired him, but that doesn't make him a murder suspect." I met the men's stares. "Does it?"

The men glanced at each other and then back at me, their expressions grim. Fluffy was first to speak, his fingers digging into his inked biceps. "He said some pretty heavy things last time he was here."

Agatha's mouth fell open as her expression turned sour. "Poppycock," she snorted. "That flaming little turd loved me like a mother, and don't you think anything else. Frankie adored me. I was his muse."

I raised my eyes to the ceiling and took a deep breath. It was pointless trying to include the delusional delight in my investigation; she was about the furthest thing possible from a credible witness. I smiled as politely as I could manage. "You should go back to whatever ghostly things you were doing before we disturbed you, Agatha. We don't need to bother you anymore. Thanks for your time." When she huffed and finally left the room, I turned my attention back to the guys. "Right, we need to get to work. Fluffy, Pus—" I screwed my face up. "Okay, I'm going to need new names for you three. I can't keep using cat names on you. Especially not yours." I wrinkled my nose as I stared at the blond man.

Pussy grinned at me and shrugged. "I don't know, I kind of like it. I don't remember my past life, but I suspect I always got a lot of—"

"I get it," I barked, flapping my hands in front of my face. "Well, there's no way I'm calling you that in public. Agatha?" I called her name loudly through the walls.

The grumpy-looking ghost returned to the room, her arms raised in surrender. "Make up your mind, for freak's sake. Do you want me here or not? I've got things to do, places to be."

I ignored her rant and smiled, jerking a thumb in the men's direction. "What were their human names, do you remember?"

Agatha thought for a long moment and then, to my relief, her expression brightened. "Yes, actually, I do."

"Well, what were they?" I prompted. The three men seemed far less concerned to know their real names than I was, for some reason. But under no circumstance was I going to call them those ridiculous pet names in front of other people. It was hard enough saying it in private, let alone having someone else witness me use the P word to address a grown man.

"I'll tell you, dearie," she cackled and her eyes filled with the sly glint of mischief. "But I'll only tell you if you promise to solve my murder."

I sighed. "Fine. I promise I'll try to help solve your murder."

Agatha wagged her finger in front of my face, frowning. "That's not good enough. I need you to promise that you'll do it, not just try."

"I can't promise that, no one can promise that," I said.

Agatha shrugged and turned to leave us alone once again. "Then I can't help you," she called as she walked through the far wall.

Groaning loudly, I surrendered. "Fine, I promise. Now, give me their goddamn names."

"Ask them," she said. I raised my eyebrows and glared at her, but the old witch merely cackled. "Just ask the big lumps, they know their own names."

My mouth hung open as a turned back to the men, glaring. They all wore expressions of amusement, and the dark-haired man gave a nonchalant shrug. "What? Maybe I prefer Fluffy to my human name."

"Maybe you'd prefer me to kick your butt than helping me figure out who the hell murdered your owner, and why you had an owner in the first place?" I said.

To my surprise, Fluffy raised one dark eyebrow and lowered his voice to a barely audible grumble. "I can think of worse things than getting my ass spanked by a beautiful girl."

Heat flooded my cheeks as he held me in his blue gaze and I whirled to the other side of the room, focusing my attention on the sweet redhead. "This is nonsense. Just tell me the names, Muffin, or I'm going to pack my bags and walk out that door without leaving behind as much as a pinch of catnip. Capiche?'

Muffin stared down at me with clear green eyes, amusement coloring his perfect features. "You do know going back to Portland won't stop you being a murder suspect, right?" I growled under my breath and he raised his hands with a grin. "Okay, okay, fine. I'll tell you my name."

"But," Pussy interrupted, his hazel eyes glinting. "You've got to earn it. Figure out the first step in your quest to find Agatha's murderer, and we'll tell you our names as a reward for coming up with a plan. *Capiche*?" He spoke the last word in a mocking tone.

I narrowed my eyes at the blond man. "You're making me earn the right to know the names of the cat people who live in my apartment?"

"Think of it as motivational," he countered.

"You know what, maybe I'll just keep calling you Pussy. Or Mr. Motivator," I grumbled. "You should be in corporate management, jackass. If you weren't an old lady's cat, that is." Something flickered behind his hazel eyes and Pussy stared down at his hands with his brows knitted together, the rare look of gravity on his face transforming his features into something sharper. I relented. "Okay, fine. The first step in the investigation is that I'll go and talk to Frankie and ask him some questions. I have Tracy's business card from the funeral. I can just visit the office and see if he knows anything. Does that plan meet your exacting standards, boss?"

The blond man's lips regained their usual curve as

he stepped toward me. "It's a bit suspicious, don't you think? You can't want to just walk in for no reason. We've all seen the TV shows, you have to be stealthy when you approach him. You need a reason to see him, so your presence doesn't make him suspicious." He grazed his bottom lip with his teeth and ran his gaze over the pink frilly robe that barely covered my torso. "And, unfortunately, he's immune to your charms."

"Well," I said, boldly returning his heated stare and extending it to include the other two men. "Lucky for me, I have three pieces of man candy who can distract him for me. So let's get down to the store and find you three something nice to wear." I smirked. "Something nice and tight that Frankie would approve of. I spotted some leather pants earlier..."

"Absolutely not." The blond man's face was a mask of indignant horror.

Blue eyes glared at me from under dark brows as Fluffy joined the protest. "Like hell you'll catch me in a pair of leather pants."

The red-haired man shifted awkwardly and I released a snort of laughter. "Okay, fine. I'll think of another plan." I crossed my arms and smiled sweetly. "If you tell me your proper names."

The red-haired man's mouth curved into a relieved grin as he raised a hand to his chest. "I'm Finlay, but you can call me Finn."

He nodded to the tattooed man who was still

glowering in response to the leather pants threat. I honestly didn't know what his problem was. From what I'd seen in the bathroom earlier, he'd look mouth-wateringly good in tight pants. I blushed at my own thoughts and focused on his deep voice. "I'm Tom."

I smiled. Finn and Tom, the names suited them. Turning my attention to the blond man, I waited for him to share his human name.

Poof

All three men suddenly returned to cat form. I shrieked and jumped back, falling sideways over the arm of the chair and sprawling awkwardly as I tried to right myself. "Holy crap, why did you do that?"

The three cats sat down, looking at each other and then turning their attention back to me. "I didn't do it," Finn said.

"God damn it." Tom's voice was a low rumble. "We mustn't have control over it." He turned his crystal glare on me. "You were the one who broke the spell this morning. Do it again. Get the spell book. Or ask Aggy."

The cat's voice was rough and hard, but the look of desperation in his stare softened my irritation at being ordered around by a scarred black cat. I raised my voice. "Agatha? Aggy! We need you," I called. "And your spellbook thingy."

"That felt weird," Finn said as we waited for the ghost to appear. He scratched his ginger fur. "I don't think I like turning back into a cat without fair warning."

I could hear Pussy purring from the far side of the room. Pussy, great. The one name I didn't catch. He lifted his head from his crotch and met my eye. "I liked it. It was kind of exciting, if you catch my drift."

"You're disgusting," I snapped. "I actually think there's something wrong with you." A wide grin spread across my face as inspiration hit me.

"Oh no, she looks way too pleased with herself," Finn's voice said from the floor.

"She looks like she's up to something," Pussy agreed.

Tom frowned and did a fairly impressive impersonation of Grumpy Cat. "Spit it out, Price."

I sat back down on the chair and leaned back with a smile on my face, finally feeling better than I had all day. "I know how we're going to approach Frankie without seeming suspicious."

CHAPTER TWELVE

"I CAN'T THANK YOU ENOUGH FOR TAKING US AND AT such short notice, Tracy," I gushed as I hauled the massive cat crate onto the counter.

Dragging three enormous cats in a box two blocks down the road was no easy feat, even for someone as fit as I was. Fortunately, Agatha had one of those wheeled moving crates in her basement and I used that to drag the massive animals to the vet to their extremely vocal and annoying displeasure.

"Don't even mention it," Tracy replied with a massive smile on her face. She looked genuinely happy to see me, and her joy was infectious. "Is there anything in particular that you'd like me to take a look at? Or is this more of just an overall check-up to make sure they're in good health?"

"Well, the truth is, I know absolutely nothing about

cats. I've always really been more of a dog person," I admitted. I glanced at the cats out of the corner of my eye. "Three male cats? It's my idea of a nightmare, to be honest. They're so loud and obnoxious."

Tracy laughed with me, nodding her head in agreement as the black cat curled his lip up and hissed through the gaps in the crate. "I'm definitely a dog person, too, but I have to admit, these three really are a sight to behold. Look at the size of them. They're three big, big boys." I avoided Pussy's stare as he stretched his back and purred in agreement. Tracy bent down and peered into the crate at the three cats squished together and inside. "Why don't we bring them in the back so we can let them out of this tiny space? They can stretch their legs a little bit and I can get a better look at them."

"Sounds great, but maybe we can get some help moving this darned crate. I nearly threw my back out bringing them here; I wouldn't want you to get hurt because of these guys." I leaned to the side to peer around the corner of the room, through the door behind the front desk. Frankie wasn't at reception, but I hoped maybe he was somewhere in the back. "Do you have anyone else working with you today?" I made my voice sound as innocent as possible, though I was already sweating buckets and felt slightly sick to my stomach. The whole concept of being on an undercover investigation made me feel exceptionally nervous, despite the fact that I was really only there to ask a few questions.

Tracy positively beamed at me. “Great idea, Frankie can take care this. Frankie?” She called his name and a man I recognized from the service in the park sauntered into the room. He was tall and slim and was wearing clothing that looked worth nearly as much as the house I now lived in. When Tracy motioned for him to pick up the crate, he looked none too impressed.

“Hi, you must be Frankie,” I said as I reached my hand toward him. He took it reluctantly and shook it, offering me a quick flash of teeth. “I’ve heard so much about you.” I immediately regretted saying that. All three cats responded in warning, and I coughed loudly so that hopefully no one else caught their mewls of protest. I added quickly, “I mean, I’ve heard you used to work at the vintage shop where I live. I love the display you had in the window, it’s beautiful. Guess it must’ve been an interesting place to work, huh?” I felt a flush creep up on my cheeks as I tugged at the handle of the crate, flustered.

Frankie tipped his head to one side. “That’s for sure. So many stories I could tell you from working in that place for as long as I did, not that you’d believe half of them,” he said, a dimple flashing in his right cheek. “Here, let me help you with that.” He picked up the massive crate and awkwardly hauled it through to the back room.

I followed, but Tracy hung back slightly and nudged me with her elbow. "How are you settling in? Is everything okay? I'm really glad that you stopped by." Her voice was hushed as she spoke, as if she didn't want Frankie to overhear our conversation.

I smiled up at her and shrugged. "To be perfectly honest, things are a bit strange. I'm settling in, though. The place is starting to grow on me."

"I'm glad." Tracy smiled. "We'll have to maybe grab that coffee sometime if you do decide to stay."

"For sure, that sounds nice," I agreed. "If we both survive this check-up, that is. Who knows what kind of food Agnes has been feeding them or what kind of care they've been under. I want to make sure they're healthy and haven't been living off moth balls or anything. You should see the crazy stuff in that old house."

Tracy laughed as we entered the room with a red-cheeked Frankie struggling to lift the crate onto the high veterinary exam table. Tracy and I ran forward and helped him lift it, and when the door was securely closed, I undid the latch and let the three cats crawl out and stretch. By the looks they gave me, I knew they were none too thrilled to be crammed into such a small crate together. I was quite impressed by my brilliant idea, if I was honest with myself, but they didn't seem too keen on it. Whatever. It got us in here, and that's all that mattered.

"I'll leave Frankie in here with you to get their

weights and set up their files while I go check on a little guy next door who should be coming round after this morning's surgery." Tracy gestured at her crotch and made a snipping gesture, and Tom snarled and scampered under a cabinet. The vet eyed him curiously as she turned. "I'll be back in a few minutes, okay?" She picked up a pile of papers from the far desk, winked at me, and then turned to leave us in the room alone.

I felt a thrill of satisfaction as the door closed. Perfect. Everything was going exactly as planned. I rested my hip against the examining table as Frankie got to work with the cats. He had a way with animals, it seemed, but his innate distaste for getting fur on his clothing was quite hilarious to watch as he maneuvered the cats at arm's length from the table to the weighing station in the corner. He raised a brow as he dropped Pussy onto the scale. "The other two seem okay, but this one looks a little chubby, doesn't he?" Pussy's eyes narrowed into hazel slits as Frankie reached to squeeze a roll of the cat's flesh. "Are you a little lardy cat, huh? Too many tootsie rolls from Agatha since I left, right?"

"Did anyone tell you their names?" He asked as he sat on the rolling doctor's stool and slid over to the computer to begin setting up their files.

"Uh, yeah," I lied. "Agatha's old friends dropped by this morning and told me who everyone was. The big scruffy black one is Fluffy, the ginger is Muffin, right?" I asked, trying to sound casual. I paused and eyed the cats, suppressing a laugh. There was no way in hell I was going to speak Pussy's real name aloud. "And I'm changing the tabby's name to Pumpkin."

Frankie spun on the stool to face me, his eyebrow raised as he chuckled. "You didn't like Agatha's choice of name for him?"

I shrugged as I joined in with his laughter, releasing the tension that had been building since I arrived. "Yeah, not so much. I can't exactly picture myself standing on the doorstep and hollering for Pussy last thing at night." Frankie's face creased and tears of amusement welled in his eyes. I smirked. "Maybe Agatha was trying to tell somebody something? You never know what might have been going on with a lady like Agatha Bentley."

"You can say that again," Frankie muttered before returning to his computer to hammer away at the keys.

I took a deep breath and tried to look casual. I was cool, calm, and collected. "So, Frankie," I croaked, clearing my throat. "Thrift store worker to veterinary assistant, that's quite a career change?"

Frankie nodded, eyes fixed on the computer screen. "I trained to be a veterinary technician straight out of college, but I left Tracy's to follow my dream to be a fashion blogger. When that… didn't work out, Tracy was kind enough to take me back."

"So, you were working for Agatha while you blogged?" Frankie's fingers froze on the keyboard. I rushed on, the words falling from my lips in a breathless jumble. “What was she like? I mean, here I am living in this dead woman’s house, and I feel bad because I didn’t even know her, you know? I’d love to get to know her better if you have any stories you’re willing to share with me.”

Frankie raised a perfectly manicured eyebrow. “Oh, I have stories all right. The stories I could tell you would make your toes crawl, girl. That woman was one loony old bat. Well, you’d have to be, I guess, to run a thrift shop like that. She always had a thousand wild tales to tell, but I honestly never knew which ones were true and which ones were made up. And the kind of things she’d bring back with her from her travels were beyond fascinating, until she stopped going anywhere.” He chatted away as he expertly tapped on the computer keyboard, setting up the three files for the cats. When he was finished, he turned to face me, his face unexpectedly solemn. “So, you really didn’t know her at all? I mean, everyone knows she left the store to a total stranger, but I thought maybe you were some long-lost relative or something? I mean, to have inherited everything from her, everything...”

Frankie’s eyes glowed with an intensity I couldn’t quite get the measure of, and I couldn’t tell if he was being sly or judgemental or if there was something else entirely hiding in the molten chocolate depths of his stare. I fiddled with the hem of my shirt, feeling the cats' attention on me as I took a moment to answer. "No, we'd never met. I lost my business in a fire a few months ago, and I parted ways with my fiancé a few weeks ago, so I just needed to get away from the city and everything that reminded me of my old life. Salem was far enough away that I could afford the bus ticket and the rent here is affordable, so I applied for every job I could find and Agatha was the first to offer me one."

"That's it?" Frankie asked. His voice was incredulous.

"That's it," I repeated. "I accepted the position of assistant manager in the thrift store, and she agreed to let me rent out her basement suite for a price I could afford, but when I arrived things weren't exactly as I had expected them to be. And that's a massive understatement." The two of us stood in silence for a long moment staring at each other, an unspoken challenge burning in Frankie's eyes. I steeled myself. "So, why did you leave the thrift shop? You were the last assistant manager, right? I was your replacement?" I swallowed the lump in my throat, uncomfortable in the newly formed tension that filled the room. Even the cats were on edge, and they walked in circles around the exam table, meowing.

Frankie reached down to pick Fluffy up, his fingers working through his thick black fur. By the expression on the cat's face, I could tell he was not too pleased with the man's hands all over him, and I suppressed a smirk as I diverted my eyes up to Frankie's, waiting for him to respond. "Yeah, I was the last assistant manager." Frankie's lip curled over the words and his tone was stilted. "And I didn't really choose to leave, so much as get kicked out. Agatha ruined my life."

CHAPTER THIRTEEN

My mouth slackened as I stared at the veterinary assistant sitting beside the examination table. My lips were dry. "Agatha fired you?"

"Fired me? No. She didn't even have the decency to that, she just made it impossible for me to work there," Frankie snapped. He pursed his lips. "You know, she called herself a manager, but she literally didn't have the first clue about running a business." Frankie released Fluffy from his grasp and started to sort through the samples of pet food on the shelves that lined the back wall. "Do you know she had thirty-three vintage Chanel purses thrown inside an old trunk when I first started working there?" He smacked a tub of dog treats onto a shelf to emphasize his point. "Thirty-three."

"She didn't know how much they were worth?" I probed.

Frankie flicked his wrist. "She didn't care. She wasn't a businesswoman. I don't know why she opened the store in the first place; she didn't even want to sell any of her stuff. She just wanted to hoard the junk she liked." His grimace softened as he rested his head against the wall. "She was happy to let me do whatever I liked with the other stuff, though—the purses and the clothes. I started dressing the windows and taking photos for my blog and things picked up with the store, and she asked me to move into the basement apartment so she wouldn't be alone in the building at night… We were a sort of weird little family, the two of us, you know?"

"Sounds nice," I said, truthfully. It did sound nice.

"It was. I haven't always had a lot of luck with family. My step-father had a hard time accepting who I was, and my mom had a hard time standing up for me." Frankie lifted his chin, daring me to challenge him. "But Aggy and me? We got along fine." He frowned. "Until things kind of blew up with my blog. People started coming from all over the country to see the displays and the store started turning a profit for the first time since she'd opened the place. You'd think that'd make her happy, right?" Frankie glared at me and I nodded my head in agreement. His jaw tightened. "Wrong. She was furious. She ordered me to shut down my blog. Said if I dared post another photo of my displays that she'd kick me out on the street so fast my head would spin."

I grimaced. "And you took another photo?"

Frankie exhaled and looked at me with tired eyes. "Hermes, Chloe, Burberry, and Dior in one single, divine outfit. I couldn't keep that to myself. Art can't be silenced."

I bit my lip. He shared his art, and Agatha took away his job and his home. And the means for him to create his art. Harsh, even by the standard I'd come to expect from the old witch. Fluffy peered at me from the corner of the room, his blue eyes intense against the black of his fur. I stared back at him in silent agreement. That certainly gave Frankie a motive. I edged closer to the veterinary assistant. "So, you left on bad terms then?"

Frankie eyed me, his expression shifting like quicksilver. "Why do you care?" I opened my mouth to answer, but Frankie stood up and folded his arms. "You think we haven't heard the rumors about Agatha's death? Are you trying to accuse me of something?"

I shook my head, taking a step backward. "No, of course not. I just want to understand her better, seeing as I'm new to town and all."

Frankie's expression was stormy. "We may not have seen eye to eye, but that old lady was basically family to me. I would never hurt her—never." Frankie's lips thinned. "Besides, if anyone around here had anything to do with it, I'd bet on it being her sleazy, money-hungry cousin, Harlow. He came to Agatha a few months ago and told her he'd found a place where she could go to retire. Wanted her to sell the store to him and move to some dumpy little retirement village, but she told him where to shove his retirement property. And considering his real estate mafia has been snapping up every vacant lot and underpriced building in town lately, maybe you should go spit your poison at him if you're looking for somebody to interrogate."

My heart hammered in my chest as he spoke. "Look, I really didn't mean to upset—"

"Well, you did. Agatha's dying before we made up is bad enough, I don't need someone coming in here and giving me the third degree as well." Frankie brushed the fur off his pants before making his way toward the door without a second glance. "I think we're done here. Tracy will be back to do the full exam. Excuse me." He left and the door closed behind him with a rather loud thud.

I nervously ran my hands through my hair, shaking my head in disappointment as I sank onto the stool. I was so mad at myself. My questioning had a gone exactly the opposite way that I'd hoped it would. "Hey, doll, you did the best you could," Pussy said as he prowled toward me. I sat back so he could jump up on my lap.

The second he made impact, a loud pop sounded in the room and a rather large, naked man was suddenly sitting on my lap. Sweet organic zucchinis. I shrieked and quickly covered my mouth with my hands, hoping

Tracy hadn't heard me from the other room. I looked down at the blond man's body as his very naked ass pressed into my lap. I blushed furiously and turned away so wasn't staring directly down at his distractingly impressive… equipment,

Footsteps sounded in the hall, and I frantically pushed him off my lap and jumped up, panic coursing through my veins. "Shit, Tracy is coming. We have to hide you. What the hell are we going to do?"

I gaped around the room, exhaling as I caught sight of a closet. Sprinting over, I pulled it open and shoved Pussy inside. Running fully on adrenaline, I sprang into the closet with him and pulled the door shut, my body pressed against his firm form in the very small space. Good thing it was dark, because my face was glowing all shades of red. "Well, this is cozy," I blurted out, more nervous than I cared to admit. Why I had jumped into the closet with him, I wasn't quite sure.

I felt his muscles tense and I raised my hands and pressed my palms against his chest, surprised by his silence. Pussy didn't strike me as the kind of guy who'd let an opportunity like this slide. "You're quivering. Are you cold?"

I could feel him shake his head, body rigid. "No, I'm really just not a fan of small spaces. No big deal. It's cool."

From the tight whisper, I suspected it was, in fact, a big deal. Crap on a cracker. "I'm so sorry, I had no idea.

You should've said something before I asked the three of you to jump into the crate earlier. I could have left you at home."

I felt him shrug stiffly as he adjusted his position next to me, the full length of his body pressed up against my side. I bit my lip and hoped that he couldn't hear my heart hammering in my chest. "It wasn't so bad in the crate. I could see out a bit through the holes. Here, on the other hand, is another story." A loud hiss and claws scratching at the other side of the closet door warned us we didn't have much time.

"Well, what do you suggested we do?" I whispered hurriedly, wondering just what the hell Tracy would think if she came into the office to see two cats and no one else. Or even more awful would it be if Tracy opened the closet and saw me hiding here with a naked man. I swallowed hard, trying to push that thought from my head. I had to think of something, fast. "Okay, it'll be fine. I'll get you out of here. We just need a plan." Before I had a chance to think, my phone rang. I reached down to pull my phone out of my jeans pocket and heat flashed over every inch of my skin as I connected with warm flesh. "Shit, sorry," I swore. "That was an accident. I wasn't trying to, you know, feel anything."

His body relaxed slightly as Pussy leaned over and whispered into my ear, his warm breath caressing my skin. "You know what, it's not actually so bad in here with you next to me," he drawled. "I'm sure you could figure out a way to distract me."

I smacked him with the back of my hand as I answered the phone, keeping my voice to the barest whisper. "Hello?" I listened to the stern voice on the other end of the phone, enquiring were they speaking to Miss Priscilla Jones. "It is, but I'm afraid this isn't a very good time."

"I'm sorry to hear that, Miss Jones, because this is Officer Bert Fitzgerald of the Salem P.D. and I need to speak with you pretty urgently with regard to a recently opened case. I assume you're still in town," he barked. I opened my mouth to whisper a reply but before I could, the officer had continued his one-sided conversation. "Good. I'll meet you at the thrift shop in ten minutes so we can discuss this further."

Without giving me the chance to reply, my phone beeped, and Officer Fitzgerald hung up. I swore again under my breath and tucked my phone back into my pocket, this time careful to avoid giving the blond man beside me any distracting ideas. Although, from the sizable pressure against my hip, I had a feeling it was far too late for that.

From the other side of the exam room doorway, the sound of Tracy's voice froze me to the spot. Heart pounding in my chest, I tried frantically to think of a way out of this mess. I was in a closet with a naked man in the vet's office. I had come in the three cats, but now only had two. An angry-sounding cop needed to speak with me in ten minutes, likely about my mistaken involvement in a crazy old granny ghost's murder, and the vet was about to step into the room any moment.

Perfect.

CHAPTER FOURTEEN

"I've got to go back into the examination room before Tracy walks in," I whispered to Pussy, but from the labored breaths coming from the large, naked man pressed against me, I knew I had to act fast. "Okay, I know you don't want me to leave you in here, but don't panic. I have a plan. I have a plan." The more I said it, the less I believed it. "I have an idea. Just trust me. Close your eyes and inhale slowly."

"I don't see how this is going to help," he panted. Despite the darkness, I could feel his attention shifting to the points where our bodies connected. "Unless you want to look for your phone again."

"Shut up." I smacked his chest and he gave a tense chuckle. "We don't have time for this, Pussy. Close your eyes, inhale deeply through your nose, hold it in deep as you can and count to three." I said a silent prayer that Dr. Lee's tactics wouldn't fail me now. "Okay, good. Great job. Now, let it out slowly through your mouth. That's it, just like that." I ran my hand down his chest as he inhaled and stroked upward as he exhaled, dropping my hand lower with each motion to encourage him to breathe more deeply.

I felt his muscles relax under my fingertips and my shoulders loosened. He released his breath in a groan as he grabbed my hand. "Unless you're sure you don't want to try my suggestion, you should probably quit that rubbing."

The voices on the other side of the wall were growing louder, and I sprang away from the heat of his body. "Okay, now keep repeating the exercise. I'll be right back."

I felt him suck in a gasp. "Where are you going?"

"I'll be right back in just a second, I promise. Stay here. I've got it covered." Before he could protest, I opened the closet door a crack and snuck out, closing it just in the nick of time as Tracy opened the far door and came into the exam room. I stood there frozen, my back to the closet, a fake smile spread across my face.

The vet waved at me. "Okay, sorry about that delay, Price. I'm all yours now."

As panic coursed through my body, my mind came to the only solution I could muster in the few seconds I had to think. "Actually, I just remembered I have to pay for parking. If you don't mind giving me two seconds, I'll be right back." I ran across the room and glided through the door that Tracy stood beside, a quizzical look on her face. Parking meter? When she knew I'd come on foot? Not to mention the fact that I'd had to leave my car behind in Portland because it was in Gerard's stupid name.

"Errr, okay. I'll look after these three cuties," she began to say, but paused. Her eyes scanned the room and I noticed her eyebrows raise. "Where's the third?"

Eyes wide, I chewed my lip as I stared at her, glancing around the room, mimicking her curiosity. "Oh, gosh, yeah. Pussy ran out the door a couple of minutes ago, I guess he doesn't like getting examined. He's probably home right now, waiting for us. Just examine the other two and I'll bring him back another day." I ran outside as fast as my legs could carry me, running past a very confused looking Frankie, and leaving most likely an even more confused Tracy in the exam room with the cats.

I prayed to whatever powers that be that she wouldn't look in the closet while I was gone. I skidded to a halt on the sidewalk outside, scanning the buildings around me. I remembered passing a bakery on my way, and I ran three doors down until I spotted it and peered in the window. I let out a deep tension-filled breath as I saw Dot, the sweeter of the two kind old ladies who had visited me that morning.

"Price, dear, so nice of you to pop in," Dot chirped from the other side of the counter as I bolted in through her front door. "Are you here for some snacks? I'm sure you need some sugar to help you through that stressful move."

Chewing on my lip to the point of nearly drawing blood, I shook my head. "Actually, I was wondering if I can borrow something from you. Do you happen to have an extra apron around?"

"An apron?" She looked confused, but her smile quickly returned. "Oh, how lovely, you cook. Are you baking something at dear Agatha's house? You know, that's probably the first time her oven's been used for baking. Agatha was the worst in the kitchen."

I nodded frantically, my breath coming in ragged gasps. "Yes, I love baking, but I'm making quite a mess. I'm in a bit of a hurry though, as I think that I might be burning something. I left my muffins behind, you see." I was rambling, my mind bouncing between baking muffins and that darned cat back at the vet's.

Dot's eyes went wide. "Oh no, we can't have any ruined muffins now, can we?" She looked nervous, just about as nervous as I felt. I watched her curiously as she frantically bounced around behind the counter, shoving a massive cookie in her mouth as she turned to reach for an apron hanging on the far wall. She handed it to me and I accepted it gratefully, promising her that I would return it immediately. She nodded at me, the cookie crumbling from her mouth as she smiled, a slight pink tinge to her cheeks. "Come back anytime, dear. Anytime at all. Happy to help you out in any way I can. Do stop by again, now. Tah."

I was almost at the door when Dot appeared in front of me, holding a second apron. It was bright pink and frilly and there were tiny sequinned sunglasses embroidered all around the edges. Dot shoved the apron in my direction. Her cheeks were red and she had a chocolate cupcake gripped in her left hand. "You should take this one," she said. She took a quick bite of the cupcake and swallowed it whole. "I made it. For Agatha, you know, before…" I watched in fascination as she polished off the remainder of the cake and brushed the crumbs off her own apron with fidgeting fingers. "I never had a chance to give it to her. It was supposed to be a joke. Aggy loved silly stuff; sequins and bows and sunglasses, but she'd never use an apron because she didn't cook. I said if I made her a sequinned apron she'd have to bake something."

Her voice caught and I gave her a sympathetic smile. "I'm so sorry for your loss, Dot, it sounds like you were a great friend."

The pretty old woman recoiled from me, her face

pale. "No, I was a terrible friend." Her voice was pained. "Terrible. I always do the wrong thing, say the wrong thing. But I never meant to be a bad friend. And I'm so sorry for how things ended. Between us." I opened my mouth to reassure her, but she vanished into the kitchen before I could say another word.

I waited for another moment to see would she return, thinking how sad it was that Dot hadn't had a chance to make up with her friends before she passed away, but she didn't appear. I turned and sprinted out the door with the apron in hand, and ran back to the vet's as fast as my legs could carry me, Dot's round face still on my mind. It was good to know that I wasn't the only ridiculously awkward person in town. Frankie looked just as confused as he had before as I came bolting back into the office. I skidded past him and through to the exam room before he had a chance to speak. I opened the door and stepped inside, half expecting to see a traumatized Tracy standing in front of a very naked man, but to my great relief she was standing next to the exam table examining the very same tabby that had been pressed against me in human form in the closet only moments before.

"This poor little guy was locked in the closet," she said to me, her voice full of concern. "He looked positively terrified, the poor handsome boy."

I caught the cat's expression and suppressed a smirk. "I'm so sorry, I have no idea how he could've gotten in there. I was sure he'd escaped out the front." Tracy's stare focused on the apron in my hand and a burning red flush of embarrassment, which seemed to be a permanent fixture on my face since I arrived in Salem, ran over my skin. I tucked the apron under the back of my shirt and gestured toward the cats. "So, how do they look, Doc?" I silently cursed myself for sounding so stupidly awkward. *Doc? Seriously?*

"Well, I've got to be honest, they're quite large for domestic cats. I'm not quite sure where Agatha picked these guys up." She paused, staring at the files on the computer screen. "Look, they're not bobcats and they're not Lynx, but I'm guessing there was some kind of funny-business involved in breeding these guys."

The breath caught in my throat as I began to follow Tracy's train of thought. My mouth was suddenly as dry as the Sahara desert. The vet gave me a sympathetic grimace and exhaled. "As far as I can tell, you have three perfectly healthy felines. But unless you can find their papers, I'd suggest you keep them indoors and away from prying eyes," she continued kindly. "But if you decide to keep them, we should probably have a little chat about neutering, sooner rather than later, okay?"

Tracy lifted Pussy off the table and turned to hand him to me, but I took a step back, knowing perfectly well what happened last time I came into contact with him. The last thing I needed was another naked man incident. Oversized wild cats were one thing, but cats that turned into ridiculously handsome men? I suspected even super-sweet Tracy couldn't be trusted with that secret. I held my hands in the air and grimaced. "You know what, I'm actually pretty allergic to cats. Do you mind helping me get them back into the crate?"

Concern filled Tracy's eyes as she looked up at me. "Are you sure you're going to be able to handle three large cats like this if you're allergic to them? If you can't manage them..."

I bit my lower lip and stared at the three furry faces watching me from the floor. I had just escaped one asshat of a man, I didn't necessarily need three more popping up in my life. But giving away three humans-turned-cats, or cats-turned-humans, or whatever the hell these three were didn't seem like the right decision. Tracy brushed my sleeve with her hand. "Do you want me to call the wildlife department, Price? I have a friend in there, a good woman, she could help."

I shook my head with unexpected strength. "No, absolutely not, I'll be fine. These were Agatha's cats and they belong in her home. It's nothing an antihistamine can't fix. But if you don't mind." I motioned to the massive crate on the ground. "I'd appreciate the help."

Tracy looked at me for a long moment and then shrugged, an easy smile returning to her face. "Whatever you say, Price." Her smile broadened. "I think you guys are going to make the perfect little family."

I scrunched my face as I watched her herd the three cats back into the crate, poor Pussy reluctantly going in last. "Yeah, something like that," I muttered. "Thanks again for seeing us, I really appreciate it. Shall I go check out with Frankie? How much do I owe you?" I tried not to flinch, thinking of the pittance left in my bank account.

Tracy brushed it off with a wave of her hand. "Don't even worry about it. It's been my pleasure. My little welcome to the neighborhood gesture."

Gratitude swelled like a wave in my stomach. "Thank you, I really appreciate it. You've been so kind, I can't tell you how much I mean that, especially with everything that's going on."

Tracy's strained smile hinted that the rumors about Agatha's death had reached her ears. "If you ever need anything, Price, you know where I am." As I took hold of the massive crate and hauled it out the door toward the front lobby, she placed her hand on my shoulder. "The offer for coffee still stands, if you're ever up for a chat or some girl time. I know how lonely it can be in a new city without any friends. You have one in me if that means anything."

I turned back to her and gave her a tight smile. "That means more than you know, Tracy. Thank you."

Moving as fast as I could without seeming rude, I

hauled ass out of the vet's office and dragged the heavy son of a bitch crate the few blocks back to the house. I swear, the journey back to Agatha's seemed twice as long then it did on the way to the vet's. I slowed as we neared the house, my eyes falling on the parked police car in front of the large three-story building. I stopped at the foot of the stairs to catch my breath, practicing my normal breathing routine to try and steady myself.

"What's the holdup, Pricetag?" Pussy hissed through the gaps in the crate, strain evident on his furry face.

I tried not to move my lips as I responded. "The cop is already outside the house."

The black cat arched his back and pressed his face against the crate as if he might be able to squeeze his way onto the street and confront the cop. "Pull it together, Price," Tom hissed. "Stop acting so nervous, because you'll definitely look guilty."

"That helps tremendously, thanks, Fluffy," I snarked. "You should be a life-coach."

Finn's green eyes blinked at me. "You'll be perfectly fine, Price. Take a deep breath and go in there. You did nothing wrong, you're innocent, and kind, and lovely. Everything will be all right."

Despite myself, I felt the knot in my stomach loosen in response to his words. I gritted my teeth. "Okay, that's enough out of you, Three Stooges. Shut up and act like cats or else Bert will have even more questions for me. Jail is bad enough, I don't want to end up being shoved in the loony bin because of you guys."

Grateful for their cooperative silence, I walked slowly and painfully up the steps to the front door, refusing to glance over my shoulder at the cop car. The same shadow of guilt I felt every time I was pulled over even if I wasn't speeding tugged at my brain. It was an illogical, but powerful response to authority that I'd had for as long as I could remember. I definitely had nothing to do with Agatha's death, but still the fact that Officer Bert sounded so serious on the phone and hung up on me made me exceptionally worried. I frowned at the front door, unlocked and ajar, and stepped inside.

The stairwell was empty, but light streamed from the open door to the apartment above. I frowned as I hauled the crate up the narrow staircase, grateful for the mornings I'd spent swinging kettlebells over my head and dragging old tires through the snow with my boot camp buddies while Gerard slept off his late nights at work.

I grunted as I reached the top step. Late nights at work my ass. "Hello? Officer Fitzgerald, you in here?" I didn't add that he was a rude, ignorant, punk for letting himself into my home uninvited. I dragged the crate into the apartment and peered into the living room. I froze. A broad, gray-haired man, who I assumed was Bert, was sitting in a chair in the front family room, twiddling his thumbs as dear old Agatha flew around him making gestures obscene enough to color my cheeks. A moment of panic overtook me before I realized he couldn't see her, but I glared at her anyway. A gyrating granny was the last thing I needed while I got grilled by Officer Fitzgerald.

"Are you all right? You look like you just seen a ghost," Officer Bert said to me as he pushed himself up off the chair. He offered a curt nod, which turned immediately into a frown. "I appreciate you coming so quickly, Priscilla."

"Price, please," I said to him, offering him a small smile. I placed the crate down beside me. I suspected that so long as I didn't touch the cats or say any magic words they wouldn't turn into humans, but it wasn't a hypothesis I was willing to test in front of a cop who thought I was guilty of murdering an old lady. No matter how cute they were as men, or how nice it would be to have them standing between me and Officer Bert's long arm of the law, opening the crate would be a bad idea. The thought of long bodily appendages brought an entirely different image to my mind and I straightened my shoulders. Get it together, Price, you're not a damn teenager. I turned to the cop. "Thank you for coming to see me, Officer. I've got to admit, I didn't expect you to let yourself in. Do you have a key? Were you and Agatha close?"

I didn't want to aggravate the cop, but it would be no harm to show him I wasn't some two-bit bimbo he could harass and bully into admitting guilt. And if he didn't have a key? Well, he'd better have a darn warrant or I'd be slapping a charge for breaking and entering on the table. The officer looked down at me with a creased brow, drawing himself to his full height. "The door was open, Miss Jones. You called for me to come in."

Behind his back, Agatha pretended to stroke the officer's shoulders, her hands creeping down his arms and toward the buckle of his belt. I let out a strangled yelp and the police officer took a step forward with his hands outstretched. "Miss Jones?"

I transformed my cry into a cough, shooting Agatha a poisonous glare, and gestured toward the crate. "Allergies, sorry. I inherited Agatha's cats, but we're not exactly compatible." The officer turned his attention to the cats as they hissed in protest, and I grabbed his arm, pulling him away from the crate before he could ask me any questions about Agatha's over-sized pets. "Of course, I opened the door for you, all this cat business has me flustered," I said in my sweetest voice. I motioned for him to sit back down as I sat on a chair across the room. "Can I offer you something to eat? Some coffee?"

He shook his head and began pacing the room, ignoring my invitation to sit. "I'm afraid this isn't a casual visit, Miss Price. I'm sure you've heard by now that Agatha's death is being investigated as suspicious. And with you turning up only days after her death, some days after she changed her will to leave everything to you, well, I'm sure you've already figured out that we're going to have to investigate your relationship with Mrs Bentley."

No beating around the bush for Bert. Awesome. I took a moment to think of a suitable response, but my mind was blank. "Look, I know it seems suspicious, officer, but I can assure you that I had nothing to do with Mrs Bentley's death. I never even met her. I was supposed to meet her yesterday to pick up the keys. I was supposed to come work for her, for heaven's sake. The last thing I expected was to show up at her own funeral with no warning. I have to admit, it was quite a shock. And now I'm being accused of murder?"

"Nobody's accusing you of anything just yet, Miss Jones." Officer Bert nodded as he rubbed his chin. "I just wanted to come in to warn you what's to come."

He stopped pacing and finally met my eyes, his expression grim. I attempted to swallow the lump in my throat as I looked up at him. "And what exactly is that, officer?"

Bert paused a long moment, our eyes locked on each other. "I'll be in touch, Miss Jones. If you're planning on leaving the city, please make sure you let us know first."

Then he turned on his heels and marched out of the apartment, the door slamming shut with a thud behind him. I let out a stress-filled breath I'd been holding, my pulse racing and my heart threatening to burst from my chest.

"I never was a fan of that chubby bastard," Agatha spat as she stuck her tongue out at the door he'd exited through.

I pursed my lips and glared at the old woman. "Really? Then do you care to explain why you invited him into the apartment and practically ghost assaulted him?"

From the crate, one of the cats made a retching sound, and I smirked in approval. Agatha scowled at the crate. "Jeez, can't a ghost have a little fun? I said I wasn't fond of him, I never said he didn't have something to warm my old bones." She gave me a sly grin. "I was always a sucker for a husky body. And a huge pe—"

"Oh, wow." I clamped my hands over my eyes and spun away from her leer. "You have a way with words, don't you?"

Agatha shrugged as she disappeared through the far wall, leaving me alone with the cats. "It's all about the audience, girlie. I don't have much to say to someone with a brain the size of a pea." Her voice echoed through the halls as she disappeared.

"Ha, my brain is the size of a pea? I'm not the one trying to ghost-grope innocent men," I muttered as I unlatched the crate. All three cats poured out at once, and one by one, they brushed up against me and turned back into human form.

"It worked. Sweet," Finn chuckled. "Now if we can only figure out what it is that turns us back into damn cats, then we'll have the whole furry issue sorted."

I pulled the apron from where I'd tucked it into the waistband of my jeans and tossed it at him, averting my eyes immediately. Or almost immediately, at least. "Okay, we've got to figure something out about the whole lack of clothing thing."

Pussy shrugged and stretched his toned body, a wide grin on his face. "I don't know; it's kind of freeing." He lay down on the sofa, lounging back and running his hands through his blond hair as if he had not a care in the world.

I stood up and stamped toward my bedroom, shaking my head as I passed Tom's inked muscles and caught a glimpse of his futile attempt to cover his essential parts with his large hands. "Find some clothes, boys. Or I'm going to let Tracy give you the snip."

I sat on my bed for a long moment and rested my head in my hands. Officer Fitzgerald's words ran through my addled brain. I didn't even know the exact date when Agatha had died, but it didn't really matter. I didn't have an alibi for any of the days I had spent on my own in the pool house after Gerard had announced he was proposing to Ivana. Unless empty bottles of organic wine would be acceptable as witnesses to corroborate my story, I had a crate full of those to prove I'd spent my first few days as Gerard 's ex-fiancée wisely. I groaned at the memory and buried my face in the pillow. I quickly wiped my eyes clean as a gentle knock sounded on the door. "What do you want?"

"It's Muffin," a soft voice came from the other side of the door. "Err, I mean Finn. Finlay. Can I come in?"

"Are you naked?" I asked.

Finn's reply was a snort of laughter and my lips curved as I imagined the amusement in those emerald eyes and on those full lips. "I found jeans downstairs in the store, but I came back up before I picked up a shirt. I can go back down and look for one?"

"Nah, it's okay. Come in." I let out a sigh and slunk back on the bed, gazing up at the ceiling above me as he eased the door open. "Might as well come join my pity party." I stared at the empty space behind Finn. "Where are the rest of the guys?"

I tried not to stare as Finn padded across the floor in his bare feet. The faded jeans were slung low on his hips, and I found my gaze drawn to the shaded lines between his defined muscles, imagining how they would feel under my fingertips. The mattress sank heavily beneath his weight as he perched on the side of the bed, rolling me a few inches closer to him. "Fluffy and Pussy turned back into cats again."

My lips curved. That stupid cat's name, it never got old. "And you didn't? Weird."

Finn shrugged, and I scooched over to the other side of the bed, gesturing for him to lie down beside me. He sunk back into the pillow and cradled his head on his arm as he turned to face me. “It’s all messed up, isn’t it?”

“A ghost, three cat-men, and an idiot who’s going to get charged with murder? Yeah, it’s pretty messed up,” I said.

Finn’s brow furrowed. “You’re not going to be charged with anything.” He reached out and brushed a strand of hair off my cheek with a fingertip as gentle as a butterfly’s wing. I held my breath as his stare landed on my lips. “And you’re not an idiot.” His frown deepened. “I don’t know what the hell is going on here, Price, or why we’re not cats anymore, or if I was ever someone else before being Aggy’s cat, but I’m glad it was somebody like you that broke the spell.” He paused, dragging his green gaze away from my lips and up to my eyes. “Somebody kind, and smart, and strong. Somebody who’ll stick around to help us figure this mess out. And maybe I’m not as smart as Fluffy, but I’m pretty certain most girls would have taken one look at us and Aggy and run for the hills.”

I rolled onto my back, away from the intensity of his stare. “Oh, man, you’ve got me all wrong, Finn. I can think of five-hundred words to describe myself, but smart and strong?” My laugh was a bitter hiccup. “But I’ll stick around, all right. I can’t exactly leave, not after what Officer Bert said; I'm not fugitive material. And Agatha deserves to know the truth." I paused, chewing on the corner of my lip. "You guys deserve to know the truth about yourselves, too."

Finn threaded his fingers gently through mine and we both stared at the evening light as it cast bands across the ceiling. "If Aggy really was murdered, somebody has to know enough to clear your name," he mused.

"Who, though? Frankie was a bust. He's probably committed a few crimes against fashion in his time, but murdering Agatha?" I raised an eyebrow at Finn and he nodded in agreement. "I feel like I'm swimming against the tide here. I am working with practically no information. Why didn't they suspect murder straight away? What changed their minds? Who else wanted Agatha dead if it wasn't Frankie?" I rolled onto my side and propped myself up on my elbow. "What about Agatha's cousin? Do you think it's worth sniffing him out or was Frankie trying to throw me off the scent?"

"Sniffing him out," Finn chuckled. I slapped his chest, surprised by the silky smoothness of his skin, and he grinned. "What? I thought you were making a cat joke."

I wrinkled my nose at him. "Okay, well, that would have been a dog joke, and I wasn't. I was asking a serious question."

"A dog joke?" Finn placed his hand over his heart.

"You wound me. And I thought we were getting along just fine." I pursed my lips and Finn raised his arms in surrender. "Okay, okay, the cousin." He stared at the wall for a moment. "I remember him. He didn't come around often, maybe once a year around the holidays. Aggy was always rude to him, but that's just Aggy. I actually think she kind of liked him coming over; she used to get all dressed up and take her rollers out before he came. But…"

His voice trailed off and he frowned. I touched his shoulder. "But?"

"They had some sort of a falling out a few months ago," he said.

I raised my eyebrows. "Over the retirement home?" I prompted. "Like Frankie said?"

"Maybe?" Finn screwed his eyes shut. "I don't think it was just the house. He wanted her to get away from the city. He said she wasn't safe here." He sat up and a sudden burst of light illuminated the forest of his eyes. "He said she was playing with fire in Salem."

"Playing with fire, eh?" I lay back into the pillows and Finn did the same. "Certainly sounds like there was something funny going on in the Bentley clan." I turned my head to face Finn and something rippled in my gut. "I'm going to find who did this, Finn. I'm going to get answers for Agatha, and find out how to break your spell and give you your life back, and then I'm going to open my damn juice bar."

"Atta girl," Finlay said as he stroked my cheek with his large, warm hand. "Not just a pretty face," he murmured, and for the thousandth time that day, I felt my skin turned red.

This time, I didn't care.

CHAPTER FIFTEEN

I MUST HAVE FALLEN ASLEEP, BECAUSE I WAS WOKEN BY soft rays of light from the rising sun flitting through the bedroom window. I yawned, stretched, and allowed myself to relax for a blissful moment. I couldn't remember the last time I had slept so soundly. It had probably been years before, back when Gerard and I had first started to share a bed and I felt like nothing could ever harm me as long as I was in his arms. The stupid, naivety of youth.

I tensed, suddenly aware of the warm presence at my side. Holding in a shriek, I eased to one side as I turned to see Finn lying beside me, naked from the waist up. His arm was draped across my side and his perfect features were angelic in the morning sun—nose straight, jaw strong, full lips balanced by dark brows and lashes, all topped off by that short auburn hair. He was beautiful, no doubt about it. Pity he was a part-time cat.

I slid out from under his arm and tiptoed across the room, careful not to wake him. Fueled by a newfound energy, I rooted for a towel and some fresh clothes. This was it. This was the day I took control of my sorry life. I would hunt down Agatha's cousin and find out what the hell he knew about her death, and I'd bring all the evidence back to Officer Fitzgerald and clear my name so I could open my new smoothie bar and start a whole new life. Who the hell needed Gerard and his yogalates and money? I was a strong, independent woman, and I was taking control of my destiny with no man to hold me back.

"You know, you could make a guy feel pretty cheap by sneaking off without saying goodbye." I dropped my towel at the unexpected sound of Finn's teasing voice and he yawned lazily, stretching his long arms over his head, every muscle in his body rippling.

I forced myself to keep my eyes fixed on his face, refusing to let my gaze wander. "Sorry, I didn't want to wake you." I picked my towel up and held it in the air. "Just taking a shower."

The door swung open and a mussed blond head appeared. "Shower? Is that an invite?"

I crossed my arms over the soft pink towel, holding it to my chest. "Well, well, look what the cat dragged in. No tail today, Pussy?"

"Meow, look who has her claws out this morning," he purred. "I love it when you're feisty."

Shooting him my best attempt at an evil glare, I slipped into the en-suite bathroom and turned full circle, searching for a shower. I emerged a minute later to find Pussy and Finn engaged in some sort of wrestling match on my bed. I raised my eyebrows and cleared my throat to get their attention. "Okay, firstly, stop that weird cat-fighting thing you're doing. Secondly, is there a shower in the main bathroom?"

"It doesn't work," Pussy said, flopping down onto the bed beside Finn. I stared at the skin-tight red underwear he was wearing for a moment and he gave a throaty laugh. "Like what you see, Pricetag? You're always welcome to get a closer look if Muffin hasn't worn you out after your night together."

I flung my towel at his barely covered crotch and gave him a middle-fingered salute. "I'd rather suck lemons than get anywhere near your weird little panties, creepbag, and all that happened in this bed was two people sleeping like babies. Thanks for your overzealous interest." I tapped the floor with my bare foot. "Now, seriously, where's Aggy's shower? I smell like cat."

Pussy rolled off the bed and draped the towel over my shoulders like a cloak, brushing my hair to one side with firm fingers. His grin seemed to slide over my skin as he sauntered past me. "I wasn't joking about the shower. There's one in the main bathroom but it doesn't work." He paused on the threshold and glanced over his shoulder. "I guess I could mess around with it later and see if I can get it working. I'm sure you could think of a way to pay me for my service…"

Before I could fling anything else at him, he disappeared into the corridor, red satin clad buttocks winking at me with every step he took. I huffed to myself in irritation as I stamped into the bathroom and twisted the faucet on the tub. Finn dragged himself off the bed, that easy smile of his plastered across his face. "Don't let Pussy get to you; it'll only make him want to tease you more."

"I know, I know, he just gets right under my skin. I've no idea how you and Tom put up with him for so damn long, I'd have smothered him in his sleep," I grumbled.

Finn grinned. "Don't let Officer Bert Fitzgerald hear you saying things like that."

"Very funny," I said, watching his reflection in the age-stained mirror. I hugged my arms to my chest. "What Pussy said—we just fell asleep, right?"

Finn's skin flushed across his cheekbones. "Of course, you fell asleep on my arm before we'd even finished talking about Agatha's cousin. I'd never have stayed otherwise, but I didn't want wake you." His mouth curved at the edges and he glanced at me out of the corner of his eye. "And maybe I kind of knew the guys would be a little jealous if I got a chance to sleep in your bed and they didn't," he admitted. I raised my eyebrows. "Sorry, Pussy was just so pleased with himself because he had his seven minutes in the closet with you; I don't usually get a chance to get one up on him."

I took a step closer to examine his face. "You're younger than the other two, right? Only a few years out of college?"

A look of puzzlement crossed Finn's face and he ran a hand through his short hair. "I think I'm the youngest," he mumbled. "It always feels that way at least. But I was the first to get here." He screwed his eyes shut for a moment. "I was Aggy's first cat. I was alone here for a little while until Tom arrived. Pussy came last."

I snorted. "Oh, wow, there's a mental image I could have done without." I wrinkled my nose. "Can you please not use that name, especially not in that sentence."

"You don't like to think about Pussy coming last?" Finn asked, widening his eyes in faux innocence. "You'd rather if Pussy came first? Because, honestly, I think he'd like that better, too."

I leveled a punch at Finn's defined bicep, flashing him a self-satisfied grin when he rubbed his arm in surprise. "Watch your filthy mouth, young man. I wasn't even trying to hurt you that time."

"Okay, point taken, no more pussy talk." Finn ducked my punch and skittered out of the bathroom, gesturing to the tub. "You better turn the faucets off before you flood the apartment. I'd hate to see Pussy come in here and get all wet."

I slung my hair elastic at him, just narrowly missing his denim-covered butt as he slipped into the corridor. "You think you're really funny, don't you?" I called after him. He grinned over his broad shoulder at me like he *knew* he was really funny, and I let my face collapse into a smile. "Hey, Finn, what's his real name, anyway?"

Finn shrugged and twisted his perfect body so that he was walking backward into the living area. He spread his hands and gave me a lopsided smirk. "No can do, Price. Not my name to tell. You're going to have to find a way to get that little tidbit out of Pussy yourself." His grin broadened. "And I bet he's going to make you work for it."

I leaned my weight against the doorframe and watched Finn disappear into the living area. I laughed softly to myself. "Yeah, I bet he is."

CHAPTER SIXTEEN

THE HOT BATH WAS EXACTLY WHAT I NEEDED TO RINSE away the stresses of the day before, and I stepped out of the bathroom a new woman. I walked into the main living space to find the three men lounging casually, all dressed in the most ludicrous attire imaginable. I gaped at them each in turn, their outfits ranging from 1920s dapper-wear to ridiculous sequined numbers from the 90s. "You look ridiculous, all of you. Where did you find this stuff?"

Pussy gave me a slow turn, a wide smile on his face. "You do live above a thrift shop, you realize?"

Tom's voice was a low grumble. "You own a thrift shop, actually."

I eyed him and crossed my arms. "So, what you're saying is that you stole from me, then?" I forced a look of mock rage on my face, which slowly turned into a smile when I saw the amusement glint in his eyes. Hallelujah, praise the lord, the black cat had a sense of humor after all. I turned away from him, suddenly flustered.

"Is she blushing again?" Pussy asked, looking from Finn to Tom. He stared at me. "Stop blushing, princess, you need to conserve your energy if you're going to figure out who killed our Agatha."

"Did someone say my name?" The old witch swept through the wall and into the center of the room with a flourish. "You guys planning a party or something?" She floated over to the couch beside Pussy and sat down next to him in her frilly nightgown and fuzzy slippers, looking equally as ridiculous as the rest of them. "My, my, don't you scrub up nicely, boys. If I was a few years younger—"

"And not a ghost?" I suggested. "And they weren't your cats?"

"Semantics, semantics." Agatha gave me a sly look. "Besides, they don't look very catty right now, do they? They look positively delectable."

I stood and stared at the men for a long minute, the shadow of a thought niggling at the base of my skull. When it finally dawned on me, I pursed my lips and turned on Pussy and Tom. "You guys are back in human form." I wasn't sure if it was a statement or a question.

Tom shrugged. "Good observation, Sherlock." He

glanced at the ghost. "Your mystery is in good hands, Aggy, this one is a genius."

"Hardy-har, smart ass," I snapped, pointing a finger in his direction. "You guys turn into human form when you touch me, right?" I narrowed my eyes. "So, when exactly, pray tell, did you touch me without my knowledge?"

Tom looked the other way, refusing to meet my eye, so I turned my attention to Pussy. He simply shrugged and whistled as he stared up at the ceiling. I looked back to Finn, who also offered a shrug. "Don't ask me, I was in bed with you."

Agatha feigned an overly dramatic gasp. "Jumping into bed with my pets already? Somebody knows how to take the 'V' out of vegan, that's for sure."

I leaned forward and wagged my finger at her like a mother scolding a young child. "You mind your manners, Agatha Bentley. No slut shaming." I crossed my arms. "Besides, I didn't get up to anything with anyone. We simply fell asleep beside each other. That's it. End of story, nothing to see here." Even if Finn did have a stomach I could lick, and if Pussy's hands did feel like silk on my bare skin, and if what I'd spied under Tom's towel had made me squirm in the most unexpected way. All of that was beside the point. Agatha gave me a look that suggested she knew exactly which three points were on my mind and I turned my face away and channeled Dr. Lee. *Peace and zen, peace and zen. I'm in control of my own body. I'm in control of my own mind.*

"You look like you need breakfast," Finn said. He jumped up from the couch and marched into the kitchen. After a few seconds I heard him shout back, "What do you want? We have eggs, cheese…"

I rolled my eyes. "I'm a vegan, remember?"

"Okay, so, bacon?" His voice called back, teasingly.

I snickered as I made my way into the kitchen to join him. Jerk. "Do you have any fruit?"

I stood beside him at the fridge, but he nudged me away. "We have avocado. Does that work? And toast?" Before I could open my mouth, he held up his hand. "Dot left it on the doorstep this morning and her vegan bread is good—no whey, no eggs, no filler. The woman makes great food." His voice softened and he gave me a lopsided smile. "I used to sit on her windowsill at the coffee shop and watch her bake most mornings."

I bit my lip, something catching in my throat at the expression on his face. "Okay, avocado toast it is." I let him prod me toward the table, squeezing his fingers before he returned to his preparation. "Thank you, Finn."

Finn held my gaze, but the moment was ruined by Agatha flinging herself onto the chair beside me with a groan. "Avocado toast," she scoffed. "What a flaming hipster. If I looked up the definition of hipster in the dictionary, there would be a picture of you, skinny minny."

"I'll have you know, I'm strong, not skinny," I lectured her, and she mimicked my angry expression. I let out an indignant sigh and turned away from her, scowling.

The ghost muttered under her breath. "You're skinny, and you have no boobs."

"Well, you're rude and bad-mannered and probably used your big breasts and your magic to get everything you wanted in life. At least, I can say I work hard for what I have," I retorted, stung by her words and fighting the urge not to cover my chest. Gerard's voice rang in the back of my mind, suggesting the name of a plastic surgeon who could help me with my 'issue.' I'd damn well send him and Agatha to hell if I had half a chance.

"Whatever," Agatha spat. "I'm not the one batting my eyelashes and simpering at my own little harem."

My mouth fell open. "I do not have a harem! I just told you I didn't sleep with any of them." I turned back to the two men lounging casually on the furniture. "And I still want to know how you both turned back into human form."

"Harem hussy," Agatha coughed.

"I quite like the sound of that," Tom said, grinning slowly.

"Only, it wouldn't be a harem," Pussy added. "Maybe like a backward harem or something."

I pressed my hands to my ears as my eyes nearly bugged out of my face. "What is my life even right now?"

Tom smirked. "A reverse harem?"

This conversation wasn't happening. "Who in their right mind would want to be involved with multiple men at once, huh?" I snapped, suppressing the curious surge that twisted through my core. An image of the last time I'd attempted to seduce Gerard slithered across my mind, souring the excitement in my stomach, and I cringed inwardly. I crossed my arms. "One man was bad enough, and three is far too many at this point in my life, thank you very much."

"Oh, come on, what girl wouldn't want to be surrounded by a ton of perfectly intelligent, strong, sexy men such as ourselves?" Pussy winked.

Tom's mouth lifted on one side and he flexed a tattooed arm. "Sexy shifters for the win."

I folded my arms. "Yeah, you're talking paranormal romance, and I've read that. Usually the heroes are some sort of strong, appealing beast like a lion or a bear. You guys are literally fluffy house cats."

Pussy grinned, clearly enjoying this conversation far more than I was. "Sexy, sexy house cats."

"Get over yourselves," I snapped.

"You're basically living the dream of any woman who has read one of those books," Pussy drawled. "A naughty little living dream."

"I'm going to wake up tomorrow in a psych ward and this is all going to be a dream," I groaned in agreement. "Or a nightmare, rather. I just know it."

"Besides," Pussy added as if I hadn't spoken a word. "You're getting three cats for the price of one. You should feel privileged."

I muttered, "I'm more of a dog person."

Agatha sneered. "Whiney little hipster hussy."

"Aggravating crass-mouthed granny ghost," I sniped.

"Did someone order avocado toast?" Finn chimed in as he stepped in between us with a plate of food in his hand and a rather satisfied grin on his face.

"Just what the reverse harem ordered," Pussy teased. I grabbed the plate from Finn with whispered thanks and took a bite of the damn toast, ignoring the rest of them while I chewed, and pretending not to notice the glaring irony that I was standing in front of them eating the one food that was the root of all hipster jokes. And it was absolutely delicious.

I swallowed a bite of wholesome goodness and pointed a finger at Agatha. "Listen, do you want me to solve your murder or not?" Agatha sighed but raised her hands in surrender. "Right, that's what I thought," I said. "So, what can you tell me about your cousin and his real estate empire?"

CHAPTER SEVENTEEN

"THAT SLIMY GEEZER?" AGATHA SCOFFED, BUT HER exasperated expression quickly fell into one of resignation. "What exactly would you like to know?" Agatha settled herself next to Tom on the couch, slinking back into the cushion, and for the first time since I arrived, looked like she was willing to have a decent conversation.

Interesting. "So, you're not on good terms with him, then?"

"Harlow is nothing more than a bag of beans. I wouldn't want to get in the way of him and a business deal," Agatha snarled. I opened my mouth to ask her to elaborate, but her voice softened. "He's not all bad, though. The chubby little gollum has his mother's heart, even if he does everything in his power to hide it behind that thick hide of his."

Finn settled himself on the arm of my chair and I leaned into him, resting my elbow on his knee. "Dot said you came to Salem to live with your aunt, was that Harlow's mother? Where did you live before Salem?"

Agatha's eyes were narrow slits. "I was born in New York City, but I got bounced around a bit before his mother took me in and brought me to live with her and Harlow in Salem. I was sixteen."

I hesitated, aware I was on shaky ground. "Did your parents come with you to live with Harlow and your aunt?"

Agatha's nostrils flared. "Dorothy Murphy has no right to spread my personal business all over town." She sprang to her feet and began pacing the floor, muttering to nobody in particular. "Doughy little busybody, poking her nose in where it's not wanted. I can do whatever I want with my life, it's no concern of hers or Bianca's or damn Harlow's, they can all go to hell." She spun to face the window and glared into the street. "I should have never come back to this one horse town. Should have stayed in New York and raised hell like I could've."

Agatha's head twisted at a sickening angle as she twisted to look at me, and for the first time since I'd arrived in Salem, I saw Agatha for what she was. A ghost. A woman without a life or a full memory or the peace to move on. Finn's arm wrapped around my waist and he pulled me against his side. Tom and Pussy both eased off their chairs and moved forward a little, standing somewhere between Agatha and me. The ghost's lips curled back. "I could have been the baddest witch this country has ever seen. I could have brought the world to its knees."

I felt Finn's fingers tighten around my waist and pressed myself against his side, grateful for the comfort of his warmth as I steeled myself to continue. I inhaled. "So, why didn't you do it? Why come back to quiet little Salem and your store and your doll-making friends?"

Agatha glared at me for the longest moment until the rage seemed to seep from her body, leaving her deflated and bowed. She shook her head. "I don't know," she muttered, turning back toward the window. "I don't know. I guess a spider just follows that silvery thread home, doesn't it?"

Tom's eyes met mine and I held his stare for a moment before nodding. He walked across the room and stood beside the old lady. Agatha was dwarfed by his large, lean frame, and despite the weight in the air, my lips twisted at the sight of them together; him in his dapper suit with his hair waves combed to one side like a gangster in twentieth-century Chicago, and her in her fuzzy slippers and robe. His voice was softer than I'd ever heard it before. I squeezed my lips together as I watched him bend his head to meet her eye. "Aggy, we're trying to help you, girl. If resolution is what you need to find your peace, you got to let Price help you find those answers. You've got to work with us, Ag." He raised one hand to her cheek, as if he could stroke her wrinkled skin. "We want to make the pain go away."

I turned my face away and pressed it against Finn's shirt. Life was a shit-show when it came down to it, but at that moment, I prayed all the people I loved would find a way to make their peace before they died. Before it was too late and they had to live with their regrets for all of eternity, because that was a torture very few people deserved. Pussy's voice dragged me from my reverie, his tone sincere for once. He gestured for Agatha to sit on the couch. "Harlow?"

Agatha nodded gently and hobbled back across the room, suddenly less wicked specter and more broken woman. She sank onto the sofa. "Yes, Harlow is my cousin. Yes, I moved in with his mother and him when I was sixteen. Harlow was only fourteen at the time, but he had ambition, even then. His mother was a widow and she'd had to work hard for every nickel and dime, and Harlow wasn't going to spend his life like that, no matter what. I left Salem for London when I was eighteen." My eyebrows peaked, but Agatha shushed me with her hand. "Another story, another time. Harlow left Salem two years later to find his fortune. Worked his way from sales clerk, to sales manager, to realtor, to property developer. He was a wealthy man by the time he settled in Salem, Massachusetts, and once aunt Sissy was gone, he only came back once or twice a year to check on her old house and make sure the tenants were keeping it right. He had no interest in this little city once he'd found the real Salem."

"The real Salem," Finn huffed. "What a swizz."

I patted his hand, surprised by his town pride, and reminded myself to tease him about it later. "If he loved Massachusetts so much, why is back in Oregon?" I asked. "Why leave?"

Agatha frowned. "Oh, he had some cockamamie excuse about wanting to come home and reconnect with his old haunts, but I'm pretty certain there were some business shenanigans involved. He probably swindled the wrong buyer and had to scoot out of Massachusetts with his tail between his legs."

I glanced at Finn over my shoulder before I asked the next question. "Finn and Tom thought you guys might have had a little falling out over something? Maybe he wanted you to move out of town?" I paused. "Said you were playing with fire in Salem?"

Agatha made a face. "Typical Harlow; trying to boss me around like I'm the kid cousin, ha. He was always on my case to move out of town and into some village for old fogeys. Thought Salem had become too dangerous for me."

I stared out the window onto the quiet, peaceful, pretty street and raised my eyebrows. "Salem? Dangerous? What made him think that?"

"I guess…" Agatha snapped her mouth shut and opened it again like a goldfish. "I don't know," she said eventually.

I shared a look with the three guys. Another hole in Agatha's memory. Interesting. I threaded my fingers together. "Do you know where I could find Harlow, Aggy? I'd like to talk to him, see if he has anything to tell us that might help." Or if he murdered you in cold blood hoping to inherit your home, I added mentally. The look on the men's faces told me I wasn't the only one thinking the worst about good old Harlow.

"He bought the big Green Victorian, right in the middle of Mission Street. Can't miss it, the fool painted it bright pink," Agatha said. She heaved herself off the couch, her usual energy beginning to surface. "He bought another place, too, a couple of hours out of town in Newport. Wanted a sea view. The address is in my notebook on the hall table." She gave me a sly grin. "You'll find it easy, little miss snoopy pants." And without so much as a goodbye, she was gone, vanished into thin air. Charming.

I huffed a loud sigh and crossed my arms, turning my attention back toward the three men who seemed far more amused than anyone had any right to be. "Okay, Mission Street and Newport. I'm guessing I should try Mission Street first. Anyone have any idea where that is?"

Finn smiled and nodded. "Yeah, it's about three

miles from here, and if you want to get to Newport and back today, you'll definitely need a car."

Pussy grinned lazily. "Why don't you just take Agatha's car?"

"Agatha has a car?" I asked before I turned to face the far side of the room where Agatha had vanished. "You have a damn car?"

Agatha appeared in the doorway, looking smug. "Of course, I have a car. What do you take me for, a peasant?"

"Well, thank you for failing to mention that before I hauled that heavy-ass crate all the way to the vet's. You're a sweetheart." I turned back to the three men and glared at them. "And why didn't any of you mention anything, either?"

"You said you loved to exercise, right? Cardio-weight training combo, pretty sweet, like, workout, no?" Tom kept a straight face, but the barest hint of a grin flickered at the corner of his lips.

Pussy raised his arms above his head and leaned back casually, eyeing me with his sharp stare. "Plus, cats don't like cars. Most animals don't, really," he added.

I turned to Finn who just gave me an apologetic grimace. "Cars really suck for cats."

I raised my hands high above my head in surrender and turned to storm out of the room, completely fed up with their nonsense. "Yeah, well, you're men, not cats." I called back to them. "I'm out of here."

Tom covered the space between us with effortless ease and blocked my path. His eyes blazed. "You're not going anywhere without us."

"Oh, really?" I folded my arms over my chest. "Is that so?"

"Yeah, it is," Tom growled. "If Harlow is capable of killing Aggy, it's not safe for you to face him alone."

I pursed my lips. "Firstly, he's an old man. Secondly, she was an old woman."

"Agatha wasn't just any old woman, Price." Tom took a step closer and his hard abdomen brushed against my arm. His eyes were as blue as the ocean during a storm. "I know you don't want to hear any of this witch shit, but it's true, whether you like it or not. Agatha wasn't some defenseless old broad. And we still have no idea how she was murdered, Harlow could have shot her with a poisoned dart from ten feet for all we know."

I dragged my gaze away from his brooding eyes and took a step back to find Finn and Pussy had closed in on me. I slithered between them with my hands raised. "Okay, guys, thanks for the protective house cat routine, but I'm pretty certain I'm woman enough to tackle Harlow." Finn opened his mouth to argue with me, but I cut him off. "Stop, no arguments. This is my life, my reputation, and my mess to sort out, okay? But if you do want to help me..."

"We do," Pussy blurted out. Tom and Finn looked at him with a level of surprise on their faces that matched my own. Clearly, I wasn't the only one who hadn't figured leering Pussy for a boy scout. He shrugged one shoulder. "What? I've got nothing better to do now that I can't lick my own—"

"Yeah, we get it." I smacked my hand over his mouth and he licked my palm in a long, firm stroke. I snatched my hand back. "You're disgusting."

"You're welcome," he purred.

Tom stepped between us with a stony expression. "What do you want us to do?"

"I need you to find out everything you can about the case. I want to know what the murder weapon was, why the cops didn't call the death as suspicious before now, what people are saying around town, basically anything you kind find out," I said. The three men nodded and I held up my hand. "But, seriously, you need to change into normal clothes first. No more playing dress-up. We have no idea where or when you guys came from, so you need to keep a really low profile in case somebody recognizes you as the local serial killer or something."

Finn frowned. "Can we please not assume we were criminals? I really don't think I was a criminal."

A smile tugged at my lips as I examined his earnest eyes. I really didn't think he had been a criminal either. My gaze slid to the right and connected with Tom's ice-blue glower. That guy, on the other hand… I pointed my finger at the three men. “Just be discreet. I don’t need you three messing everything up for me.”

Pussy saluted. “Yes, ma’am, your reverse harem won’t let you down. We know you’re relying on us to solve the case.”

“Please,” I snorted. “I don’t need any men to help me get the job done.” I gave him a derisive once-over as I sashayed toward the front door.

“Sure thing,” Pussy called after me in his sarcastic drawl. “Enjoy hot wiring the car.”

I paused in the doorway, refusing to turn back to them. After a long moment of awkward silence, Finn said, “In the hall table. Beside Agatha’s address book. With Harlow’s address in it...”

I marched down the hall and snatched the keys and the address book, shutting the drawer with a loud snap. “Thank you, jerkholes,” I muttered to myself when I was sure they couldn’t hear me.

“You’re welcome,” the three men all called back at once. I slammed the door behind me.

CHAPTER EIGHTEEN

I WAS STILL MUTTERING AND CURSING MY THREE NOT-so-feline friends under my breath when I shoved the door to the back lane open. I scanned the cracked asphalt until my gaze landed on a large object covered with a tatty old tarp. "Great." I stamped past the brightly painted wall and the strings of fairy lights, which I assumed were Frankie's handiwork, and tugged on the corner of the heavy cloth. "Let's get this old clunker on the road…" My voice trailed away to nothing as the tarp fell back to reveal a gleaming, bright red Mercedes-Benz convertible. "Holy crap," I breathed. "Not bad for a granny-mobile, that's for sure."

I hopped in the driver's seat and turned the key in the ignition, reveling in the purr of the powerful engine. A wide grin spread across my face; if I was going to drive across town chasing after murder suspects, I might as well do it in style. I wrapped my fingers around the soft leather steering wheel and grimaced. Minor problem: I had absolutely no idea where I was going.

Too stubborn to ask the boys, I pulled out my phone and did a quick Google search to orient myself towards Harlow's place, and then I was on my way. Traffic was light so it only took a few minutes to reach Mission Street. I circled the block a few times before spotting an exquisite Victorian mansion, freshly painted a bright shade of pink with a violet trim. I cocked an eyebrow as I eased the convertible into a vacant parking space; seemed like Agatha wasn't the only one in her family who had a taste for over-the-top extravagance. I patted the car's glossy red hood and made a silent promise that I'd bring it for a proper drive real soon before I straightened my shoulders and made my way toward Harlow's colorful abode.

A massive, lion-shaped metal knocker hung on the oversized violet front door. I took in a deep breath and knocked it three times, my heart racing in my chest as I waited for someone to answer. I jumped when not two seconds later the door cracked open and a short, silver-haired man appeared on the other side of the threshold.

"Whatever you're selling, I'm not interested." His voice was hushed and hurried, and he pushed the door closed before I had a chance to respond.

Seriously? I knocked again, and the door opened another crack. "I said, I'm not interested."

This time I was ready, and when he pushed the door closed I held my hand out to keep it open. "I'm not selling anything. My name is Price Jones, I'm looking for Agatha Bentley's cousin."

The door remained still for a second, and then opened fully, revealing the man I assumed to be Harlow. He had an interesting face, not handsome exactly, but captivating all the same, his icy blue eyes pale and eerie against the silver of his combed-back hair.

"Pardon me?" His gaze remained fixed on my face, yet I had the unnerving feeling that I was still somehow being examined from head to toe. Like a jewel being inspected by a jeweler to determine its worth.

I was almost certain I was standing in front of Agatha's cousin, but a little voice in the corner of my mind urged me to be cautious. I cleared my throat. "Excuse me, I'm looking for a man called Harlow Bentley, and I was told I might be able to find him here?"

The man's silver eyebrows rose as he looked up at me. "Oh? And who might've told you that?"

I paused. "Er…" I couldn't exactly say the ghost of old Agatha Bentley from the thrift store on Commercial. "Just, you know, some people. Somebody at Mrs. Bentley's funeral, I can't remember her name, sorry." I affected my best vulnerable simper. "It's been a pretty overwhelming few days."

After another few moments of studying me intently, the man opened the door wide and stepped aside with a flourish of his hand. "I'm Harlow, please, come inside, Miss Jones. Step out of that wretched cold breeze."

"Thank you, Mr. Bentley," I said, trying not to gape at the lavish interior of his home. The inside of the house was just as grand as the outside, and I wondered just how much money this real estate man had.

"Harlow Monroe," he corrected me. "Bentley was Agatha's married name." He closed the door and led me into a grand sitting room with a small table and two elegant chairs arranged in a bright bay window. I took the seat closest to the door and perched on it uneasily. I felt uncomfortable, like I was imposing.

I offered him an awkward smile, trying not to let the grandeur of the surroundings intimidate me. I felt the same way I used to when Gerard brought me to his business dinners; plain and cheap. I fumbled for something to say. "I didn't realize Agatha was married."

The expression that flitted across Harlow's face was so subtle that it vanished before I could put a name to it, but I watched closely as he pulled a handkerchief from his jacket and ran it over his mouth. "Yes, Agatha was married for a brief time in her youth." He glanced out the window for a moment. "The marriage didn't last, unfortunately, but Agatha kept the name. She thought it suited her." I smiled. Typical Agatha. Harlow narrowed his eyes and leaned his weight on the small polished oak table that lay between us. "What do you want from me, Miss Jones?"

I held his stare, battling the blush creeping its way up my neck. I wouldn't be talked down to by another jerk in a fine suit. I was done with molasses and I was done with pussy-footing around. "I just moved to town. I was supposed to work for Agatha at the thrift shop. I arrived the day of her funeral."

Harlow arched one silver eyebrow. "I know who you are, young lady. You're the girl that Agatha left her estate to."

I lifted my chin. "Yes, I am, Mr. Monroe, and quite frankly, I'm having a difficult time understanding why." Harlow slid back in his chair a little, his mouth slightly parted. "I initially assumed maybe she didn't have any family, but…" I motioned toward him and raised my shoulders in a soft shrug. "Here you are. Which, as you can imagine, puts me in a very awkward position." I folded my hands on the table. Agatha had seemed convinced her cousin had a lamb's heart, but if he did, he was a lamb in snake's clothing. And if there was one thing that unsettled a snake, it was straight talking. "You probably thought Agatha was going to leave the house to you."

Harlow's face split into a wide grin and the room was filled with the sound of laughter so infectious that I felt my own lips curve. The old man coughed and smacked the table in front of him. "Oh dear," he wheezed. "Oh dear, I'm sorry. If you knew my cousin you'd know why that's funny."

I drew my eyebrows together. "I would?"

The old man straightened himself and dabbed his eyes with his handkerchief. "My cousin was the very definition of contrary, Miss Jones. If you said that door was white, she'd swear up and down that it was black. If you told her she had pretty hair, she'd hack it off with a spoon just to prove you wrong. When I told her I'd buy the store and the apartment and let her move to a safe, secure retirement village..."

"She told you, you'd never get your fingers on her house," I finished.

Harlow nodded. "She'd sooner lick a cat's ass than let me get my greedy paws on the building, I think those were her exact words." I grimaced, assaulted by the unfortunate image of Agatha and the three cats. Oh god, the visuals. Ick. I forced my attention back to the silver-haired man. "Now, that's not to say I wasn't surprised when I heard she'd left everything to a total stranger." Harlow gave me another appraising glance before turning back to the window, shadows lurking behind his eyes. "I mean, I knew I wasn't getting a whiff of the inheritance, but I'd bet there were a few shocked people in Salem the day you were handed those keys."

My pulse raced, and I swallowed the lump that formed in my throat. I wanted to ask who he was talking about, but something about the set of his jaw made me hold my tongue. I decided to try flattery; it had always worked on Gerard. "This sure is a beautiful house. Do you own many homes?"

Harlow shrugged as if the exquisite Victorian mansion was unremarkable. "This is just one of many, yes. I am a collector, of sorts. Can't help myself. But I downsized to move out west, you know. Simplify life a little bit, if you know what I mean."

My eyebrows shot up at his words. If this was simple compared to where he lived before, I wasn't sure I wanted to know much more. He lived in a world an entire league above my own, that was for sure. "You seem to have quite an eye for architecture. I think Agatha's building is lovely too, or it could be." Harlow nodded, noncommittal. "Were you ever interested in Agatha's home? I mean, before she fell out with you."

Harlow made a face. "That ratty old thing? Not interested. As you can see, I have much grander tastes." He grimaced, as if suddenly remembering the apartment was now mine. "Of course, it could be renovated to make a lovely home for somebody. That street has a real up-and-coming vibe. Very hip."

I suppressed a snicker. *Hip*. Yeah, he was Agatha's

cousin all right. Shifting on the chair, I wondered could Harlow really have anything to do with Agatha's murder. I took in his portly physique and curved mustache, such a stark contrast to the hard lines of the room. I really couldn't see him having any motive to kill Agatha. He could probably buy any house in town with cash out of his own hand-stitched silk suit pocket. He didn't need an inheritance. He was a businessman, for sure, but that didn't make him a murderer. I got to my feet and extended my hand. "Well, thanks for your time, Mr. Monroe. I should probably head home."

Harlow nodded politely and stood to lead me back to the front door. I glanced over my shoulders as I passed through the entryway, once again aware of the unnerving prickle at the base of my spine. The feeling of being watched by unseen eyes. I waved curtly at Harlow as I slipped onto the front porch, releasing a breath as the door closed behind me. Just as I was about to step onto the pavement, the door opened again, and Harlow's voice called after me. "Oh, Miss Jones?"

I turned. "Yes, sir?"

"Have you spoken to Officer Fitzgerald yet?" Harlow asked, his blue eyes like quicksilver in the morning light. My throat constricted. The snake. The sneaky little snake. He'd known exactly why I was there all along. "If you want to ask anyone else questions about Agatha's will, I suggest you have a little chat with her friends, especially good old lady D'Arcy." The breeze suddenly vanished so Harlow's final words hit me like a shout before he closed his door with a resounding snap. "There's a reason I felt Agatha would be safer far away from Salem, and it was nothing to do with the price of tea in China."

I gaped at the bright violet door for a heartbeat before speed walking back to the car.

CHAPTER NINETEEN

DRIVING BACK ACROSS TOWN, THOUGHTS GATHERED LIKE pebbles at the base of my skull. There was something not quite right about the picture of Agatha's life that was being painted for me by those who knew her; it was like a familiar melody being played on an untuned piano. My head ached and I could barely concentrate on the road. I flicked my blinkers and pulled into a parking lot in front of a liquor store.

"Is noon too early for a liquid lunch?" I muttered to myself, eyeing the man carrying out a large bottle in a brown paper bag. He stumbled on the curb, almost losing his footing and I exhaled. "Yes, Price. Yes, it is. What you need to do is talk to somebody—somebody besides yourself."

To my utter frustration, the first image that popped into my mind was the three men-cats. I raised my eyebrows as I scrolled through my contacts, looking for the phone number Agatha had used in her job advertisement, and wondered was talking to your pets better or worse than talking to yourself. Finn's warm voice answered on the first ring and a smile pulled at my lips. Better. Definitely better. "Finn, you answered, I wasn't sure if you guys knew how to use a cell."

Finn's laughter filled my ears. "Yep, we're super cats. We even managed to charge the damn thing."

"Color me impressed, Muffin," I teased.

Finn gave another chuckle before a voice barked something at him in the background. I patted the steering wheel as I heard the phone switch hands, preparing myself to talk to surly Tom. "Price, where are you?"

I sat up straight and pressed the phone against my ear. "I'm in a parking lot off Mission Street, why?"

"Listen, Pussy turned into a cat again, but we used it to our advantage and he managed to sneak into the Police Department and find out a bit more about Agatha's case," Tom said.

I stared at the dashboard with my brows drawn together. "And?"

"And Agatha was definitely murdered." Tom's voice was grave. "There were lesions and markings around her neck consistent with strangulation. Very deep injuries, Price. The cops are pretty certain it had to be a man or a particularly strong woman who attacked her, but there was no sign of forced entry, no defensive injuries, no sign of a struggle in the store, nothing missing from the till. Nothing of note, well, except the jumbo grape lodged in her throat and enough force to snap her spinal cord."

I stabbed at the buttons on the car door in a desperate attempt to roll down the window. I needed air. I couldn't catch a breath. Tom called my name down the phone, his pitch rising as he began to curse. I forced myself to open my mouth. "I'm here, Tom. I'm okay." He exhaled into the speaker of the phone and I shook my head. "I just… I don't think I really believed it before. I know it sounds stupid, when I believed about ghosts and witches and talking cats, but somebody murdering Agatha?" I whispered. "How did they not figure it out straight away? I mean, they released her body and everything."

I heard the phone moving again and Pussy purred against my ear. "You doing okay, Pricetag?" A shriek sent a sharp dart of pain through my eardrum. "Watch where you're stepping Fluffy, just hold the damn phone for me so I can talk to her." Pussy came back on the line. "Price?"

"I'm still here. Deaf in one ear, but still here," I said. "Pussy, why didn't the cops start to investigate Agatha's death as suspicious immediately? I mean, it doesn't sound like it was a subtle murder."

Pussy's voice was tight as a drum. "This is where

things start to get really dark, Price. Seems like somebody was pulling strings in the police department. The coroner who was dealing with Agatha's autopsy suddenly got a big promotion out of town, and his assistant was offered a last-minute spot on a big fancy international conference in Zurich, and in between all the sudden, inexplicable chopping and changing, it seems Agatha's files just mysteriously vanished and her case slipped through the cracks."

"What?" I screwed my face up. "That's insane."

Pussy made a sound low in his feline throat. "It might be a little more sinister than that, Price. When Officer Fitzgerald noticed her file was missing, he started to dig around, and from what I overheard today, he's pretty certain somebody with a lot of money or a lot of power was trying to make the whole case just disappear."

"But they didn't succeed in making it disappear." I stared at my white knuckles on the steering wheel. "And now they don't need to," I whispered, realization hitting me like a smack in the face. "Because they have me to take the fall."

I could hear the guys' voices in my ear but I couldn't make out the words through the roar of my own heartbeat. It was real. It was all real. The ghost, the magic, the men, the murder. It was real and it was going to swallow me whole.

"Priscilla!" Tom's commanding bark cut through the

whirlwind of my thoughts and I turned toward the phone. As if he could instinctively sense that I was listening once more, he continued in a low voice. "Price, we're going to fix this. Now we know we're looking for somebody with money or power, and we're going to find them. We're going to make sure justice is done, Price. We won't let them take you down, okay? Do you hear me?" I mumbled something incoherent and Tom raised his voice. "Do you believe me, Price? I need to hear you say the words so I know you can hear me."

"I hear you," I mumbled. I took a deep breath, imagining the three guys standing in Agatha's living room. Tom with a deep furrow in his brow, Finn's green eyes brimming with worry and compassion, and Pussy, well, him with his whiskers and fur. An uncontrollable giggle swelled from deep in the pit of my stomach and burst from my lips.

My shoulders shook as tears of hysterical laughter rolled down my cheeks. I heard Tom arguing with the others. "She's still there, but I think she's having some sort of a breakdown."

"I'm fine," I cut across him. I took a deep breath. "I'm okay. You're right, we know more now that we did this morning and that's a good thing." I lifted my chin, thinking of Harlow and his quicksilver eyes. "And you're right; we're going to find this granny-killer, and we're going to nail him." In the background I could hear

Finn saying that Agatha was not technically a granny and Tom telling Finn to shut up, and I grinned. “Okay, guys, break it up. I’ll be home in a few minutes and I’ll drop by Dot’s place on the way home and pick up some lunch. Try not to cough up any hairballs before I get back.”

I killed the call and started the engine with a newfound sense of determination. I was almost at Bewitching Bites coffee shop, when I caught sight of a familiar face out of the corner of my eye. Short, bobbed, ice-white hair shone in stark contrast with her long black fur coat. I stared at the tall elegant figure as I pulled my car up to the curb, I would recognize that woman’s style anywhere.

I rolled down my window. ”Would you like a ride home, Bianca?”

Startled, she took a moment to recognize who I was before smiling gratefully at me. “That would be lovely, dear. Thank you.” I watched her reach for the door and wondered would she be upset if she knew Harlow Monroe was insinuating she had been a danger to his cousin. Bianca pulled off her gloves as she folded her hands on her lap in the passenger seat. Long, slender, elegant hands, the kind that were made for playing piano and mending dolls. Not strong enough to snap a spine. She gave me a reserved smile. “I’m just down the next right. I thought I’d take my physicians advice and go for a little stroll, but these legs of mine aren’t what they used to be; you couldn't have pulled over at a better time."

"I'm glad to be able to help." I smiled as I pulled back onto the road, thinking the exact same thing. Surely, it was serendipity that had led me straight into Bianca's path, just after Harlow had tried to send me after her. Maybe he didn't have a clear motive for wanting Agatha dead, but Harlow certainly had the money to twist a few arms in Salem Police Department. Before I could ask Bianca anything, my phone buzzed. I glanced down at the flashing screen and my stomach cramped.

Officer Fitzgerald knocking on the door, we think he's watching the apartment. Park in the lane and come in through the back door. – Finn

I quickly slid the screen off before Bianca had a chance to see the message. "Everything all right, dear?" she asked, my own discomfort obviously weighing heavily in the car.

"Just peachy," I lied. "How have you been today?"

"Oh, you know," she drawled, waving her slim hand near my face as she spoke. "Same old. Clients here and clients there. Never a day's rest for a haggard old woman."

I gave her a half-smile. "I don't think anyone could accuse you of looking haggard or old, Bianca." I wasn't lying. She looked great for her age, not a day over sixty if I could hedge my bets.

"Why, thank you, dear." Her voice was disingenuous, as if she was used to being showered with flattery. "What are you doing on this side of town? Lovely car, by the way; I pegged you for more of a bicycle kind of girl."

I wasn't sure whether to take that as a compliment or not. "The keys were left out for me in the house. I had a few errands to run," I quickly said, doing my best to come up with an excuse for driving around town in a dead woman's vehicle. I frowned through the windscreen, surprised Bianca hadn't recognized the car as Agatha's. "Wasn't this Agatha's car?"

"Oh, yes, you're right. How did I forget? Grief does strange things to the mind, doesn't it?" Bianca lifted her finger to her eye as if to dab away a tear, which I suspected was more an act than anything if my memory of Agatha's funeral served correctly. The older woman watched me from the shadow of her thick, blunt bangs. "I don't mean to intrude, but I'm almost certain I spotted this car outside Harlow Monroe's place earlier. You must have been paying him a visit, so sweet of you to check in on Agatha's cousin. Not that they were close. Not in the end," Bianca said. She skipped on with the conversation before I could interject. "Lovely house, isn't it? I'd almost pay him a visit myself to get a look inside."

Despite her casual tone, I could feel Bianca watching me closely. "Yeah, it's lovely. I just stopped by to share my condolences; I don't remember seeing him at the funeral."

"Oh, he was there," Bianca replied. "He's simply a doll, isn't he? He's recovered so well from that whole embezzlement thing he was wrapped up in not far back. But I wonder how he's getting on, really. People say it's only a matter of time before he runs out of people to borrow from. It's so sad when you see somebody caught in that cycle, isn't it? Borrowing from Billy to pay John, my mother used to say. Like a house of cards, it'll all fall down in the slightest breeze." She glanced at me out of the corner of her eye. "He must be up the wall that dear Aggie didn't leave him that place. Oh, just around this corner, dear."

I slowed to a crawl as we cruised the avenue. I took in the large houses and the expensive cars, I guessed if I picked a leaf from one of the straight trees lining the road, even that would probably have smelled like money. A black kitten jumped onto the pavement and Bianca wrinkled her nose. "How are you doing with those three cats of Agatha's, by the way? Nasty little beasts. Have you had them checked out, yet? There's a vet nearby, you know."

"Yes, I know. I took them to Tracy's yesterday, actually," I said. I tapped the steering wheel and felt a smile play over my lips. "I'm quite fond of the furry monsters, to be honest."

Bianca made a face like she had just walked in crap.

"Rather you than me, dear," she muttered. "So, you must have met Francis, then? Tracy's assistant. Shame what happened between Agatha and him. Poor boy. He had such high hopes for his little fashion blog-log thingy." She swiveled in her seat. "You know he chose all the outfits I wore to the International Conference of Dating Experts in San Francisco the week poor Agatha passed away? I was standing in front of hundreds of people head-to-toe in Chanel while she was breathing her final breath. So tragic." She paused for effect, hand on heart, before launching into the conversation again. "And did you know Francis dressed me for the City Council People of the Year Awards for the past three years running? My pictures got over a million hits on his instaphoto-whatever page. People were calling me a GILF for weeks."

I choked on a snort of laughter, turning it into a coughing fit to avoid the wrath of Bianca. She barely appeared to notice. "Poor Francis. Agatha was so pig-headed, kicking him out like that. Cutting off her nose to spite her face, typical Agatha. I really thought she'd at least make it up to him in her will, but I suppose she was stubborn to the end. Honestly, it was the last thing Francis needed after the Broadway fiasco."

"Broadway fiasco?" My eyebrows were practically touching my hairline. I was beginning to see what Tracy meant about Bianca.

The white-haired beauty swiveled to face me. "You

haven't heard?" Bianca didn't wait for me to answer before she launched into her tale of woe. "Francis was a drama major, you know. He was a pretty big deal on the Am Dram scene in high school—"

"Am Dram?" I interrupted.

Bianca pursed her lips. "Amateur Dramatics. Anyway, that was in high school, but when he got to college, things really took off for him. There was no role the boy couldn't play; he could have pretended to be my long-lost son and I would have been convinced, such a chameleon. He got himself an agent before he'd even graduated and landed the role of Jack Worthing in *The Importance of Being Earnest on Broadway*."

"Wow." Even I knew that was a big deal.

Seeing she had my attention, Bianca's voice lowered to a stage whisper—Am Dram style. "Opening night, Francis was caught in the alley behind the theatre, being earnest with a hunky cop who was meant to be on the beat. Well, the media had a field day. By the next day, his agent had dropped him, and his understudy was given the role of Jack. The understudy ended up landing a blockbuster movie the next year because of his performance in the role that should have belonged to Francis. Dejected, poor Francis came home and trained to be a veterinary technician. Tragic."

Bianca's thin lips curved into a wicked smile. "But he still has an eye for the cops." She pressed a finger to her lips as though we were sharing a secret. "Between you and me, my agency set him up with the big man in Salem Police Department and the man is besotted with young Francis. He'd do anything for him." She patted her hair. "I wouldn't be surprised if I need to get a hat for the chapel for a summer wedding. Another win for D'Arcy Dating Agency."

My stare was frozen on Bianca's face as the piece of the puzzle clicked into place inside my skull. A life twice ruined, a convincing actor, the head of police wrapped around his little finger. "Dear?" Bianca tapped my arm sharply and motioned for me to stop the car. "This house is mine."

Numbly, I pulled over in front of a beautiful white corner-lot house, built in Art Deco style. Bianca turned to me with a cheery smile. "Thank you so much for taking pity on an old woman. Don't you believe any of the nasty things anyone in town might be saying about you, you're a good girl, and you inherited that place fair and square. Don't let the rumors run you out of town, Salem is your home now." She stepped gracefully out of the car and gave me a queen's wave.

Before I could even respond, she was out the door and halfway up to her house, her feet as swift and light as a ballerina's.

CHAPTER TWENTY

To say I was overwhelmed would have been an understatement. I sat in the car outside Bianca's house for what could have been hours, lost in my own thoughts as I tried to sift through the jumble of information spinning through my mind. When I finally gathered my thoughts enough to drive, I couldn't bring myself to call into Bewitching Bites for lunch. The thought of what else I might learn about my neighbors from sweet, nervous Dot was enough to turn my stomach.

I parked the car beside a bland-looking deli, but before I could open my door, my cell buzzed inside my pocket. I frowned at the unfamiliar number on the display and answered cautiously, ready to kill the call if I heard Officer Bert Fitzgerald on the line. "Hi, Price?" A familiar voice sounded through the receiver.

My shoulders relaxed. "Tracy, how are you?"

"Fantastic, thank you." I could almost hear her easy smile through the phone. "How have you been? How are the cats?"

"They're great, thanks for asking. Driving me a bit crazy, but we're all doing just fine." I paused, uncertain how to proceed.

Tracy filled the silence. "Listen, I hope you don't mind me using your phone number from the cat's file, but there's an awesome little spot just down the road from my office and I was wondering if you'd care to meet me there? I have a feeling you'll love it."

I paused for a moment. The guys were waiting for me, and they'd sounded worried on the phone, but on the other hand, Tracy might have some information we could use. And I really, really wanted a decent coffee. "You know what? That sounds lovely. What's the name of it?"

Tracy's voice laughed through the receiver. "The Three Cats, if you believe it."

Of course it was. I shook my head. "Sounds great. I'll look it up on my phone and meet you there soon?"

"I can be there in fifteen," Tracy said. "See you then."

I sent a quick text to Agatha's phone before I started the engine, promising to return with the finest take-out lunch The Three Cat's could make. I drove back through the easy streets of Salem city, guided by Google Maps on my phone. When I arrived at the cute little cafe, Tracy was sitting in at a table in a cozy corner near the back. There was a painting of three massive black cats on the wall, and all the servers wore cute little cat T-shirts.

"Nice place." I took a seat across the table from Tracy.

She smiled at me. "I thought you would like it, the perfect place for a dog lover with three adopted cats, right?" She winked at me and I laughed. "Nice to see you again."

The waitress took my order, and in no time I was sipping on a piping hot soy matcha latte. It was pure bliss, and I closed my eyes and let myself relax and enjoy the moment. It was exactly what I needed.

"You look like you've had a hell of a day," Tracy said. She was drinking a steaming cup of green tea and watching me carefully.

I groaned. "You don't know the half of it. I swear to God, everyone in this city is nuts. I think you lied when you said they weren't."

Tracy grimaced. "Yeah, there are a lot of interesting characters around here, that's for sure, but I think you get that anywhere. Anyone in particular bothering you today?"

Unease prickled the nape of my neck as I stared at the pretty vet. Why was she being so nice to me? She was Frankie's boss. Maybe she knew Harlow, too.

Maybe they all knew each other. I lifted my cup to my lips and sipped slowly, trying to remember any of Dr. Lee's advice. I needed to keep a grip on reality. The whole world wasn't against me. Probably. "Oh, nobody really," I lied. I felt Tracy's gaze sharpen. I took a gulp of my latte and tried to think of the least incriminating topic. "Well, mainly those two old ladies that were at Agatha's funeral." I gestured for the waitress to bring me a second coffee. "Do you know them well?"

Tracy groaned. "Trust me, you can't live around here and not know them. Bianca and Dot are big characters. What have they done now?"

I drained my mug, waiting anxiously for my second cup to arrive. "Not much, really. I just ran into Bianca today and she had a few things to say about people in the neighborhood."

"Bianca has more than a few things to say about pretty much everyone, if you ask me," Tracy said.

I nodded my agreement. "So, Agatha was close with them? I didn't really get that impression from the way they were acting at her funeral."

Tracy leaned back in her chair, contemplating her answer. "When I first arrived in Salem, the three of them were inseparable. I used to see them together all the time, they were always out causing some sort of mischief in the neighborhood, like three children in grown women's bodies. Then something changed."

"Something changed?" I prompted.

"Yeah." Tracy stared into her cup for a moment before meeting my eye. "I think they had some sort of a falling out. I spotted them in Dot's coffee shop a few times, after hours when they used to have their strange little doll making sessions, and they were just bickering and picking at each other. " I raised my eyebrows and she grinned. "Even more than usual." She frowned. "Really going for it, you know?" I nodded and Tracy swirled her tea. "And then Agatha just stopped coming round. She stopped meeting the others, stopped going to the coffee shop, stopped harassing the people who came to admire Frankie's displays in her windows. Even stopped going on her trips to gather the stuff to sell in the store, she sent Frankie instead."

"That's strange," I said.

Tracy smiled at the waitress as she placed a fresh latte in front of me. "Yeah, it was really strange. And sad. Agatha wasn't an easy woman, don't get me wrong, but she was full of life before she fell out with her friends. I think that maybe Bianca and Dot feel a little bit guilty about the way things ended for their old friend. It's hard to accept you left it too late to offer an olive branch, maybe it's easier for someone like Bianca D'Arcy to pretend she doesn't care instead?"

I nodded slowly. It made sense in a terribly sad way. I closed my eyes and pressed my hands against them, suddenly drained.

"Price," Tracy hesitated. I opened one heavy eyelid.

She scratched the tabletop with her thumbnail. “I didn’t just ask you here for coffee.” I sat up straight and opened both eyes. “I don’t really know how to say this, but I felt I had to let you know.” Her voice faltered and I held my breath. “I thought you should know the cops have been asking questions about Agatha. About you.” She took a deep breath. “They came to talk to me after your visit.”

I felt my skin grew cold at her words. “You know I had absolutely nothing to do with Agatha Bentley’s murder, right?”

Tracy's eyes widened and she reached her hand out to grab mine, giving my palm a gentle squeeze. “I know that; of course, I do. It’s a ludicrous suggestion. You didn’t even know the woman was dead the day I met you at her funeral. Price, I haven’t known you for long, but I can see in your eyes that you’re not capable of anything so horrible. You’re a kind soul. You’re vegan, for God’s sake. If you don’t eat animals, I hardly think you’d be the kind of person to hurt a human being.”

“Thank you,” I whispered. The knot was still tight in my stomach, but I wanted to believe the vet was genuine. If she was, at least I’d have one person in Salem on my side. Well, four if you counted the cats, which I highly doubt I could in court. And using Agatha’s ghost as a witness was obviously out of the question, not that she remembered anything, anyway.

I disentangled my hand from Tracy’s and waved for

the server so I could order take-out for the guys, lowering my voice so Tracy couldn't hear the scale of my very non-vegan order. I turned back to her with an awkward grin. "Just wanted to get some food in case I have any more unexpected visitors." I gestured to the cat mural in an attempt to move the conversation along. "Salem is a regular cat heaven, right? Portland was full of dogs, dogs, dogs, but I literally can't move without seeing a cat around here. It's crazy."

Tracy spread her fingers wide on the table. "Right? Oh my gosh, I've said the same thing to so many people. It wasn't like this when I first got here. It happened a couple of years ago. Suddenly, there were just dozens upon dozens of stray cats everywhere. I don't know if a shelter opened their doors or if one of the big pharma companies is up to something fishy, but it's been a big problem lately."

The server arrived with my box of take-out and I asked for the tab, waving Tracy's money away. "Hey, you saw my three cats for free, I think a cup of tea is the least I can do."

As we left the café, Tracy nudged my arm and I turned to face her. "Price, I don't know what's going on in Salem right now." She sealed her lips for a moment and glanced over her shoulders before continuing. "But something is. And it's not good. So, just mind yourself, okay? Be careful, be smart. You seem like a nice girl, and you don't deserve to be messed up in anything strange, okay?" I nodded at her, thinking she had no idea just how strange my life already was. Tracy began to walk away, but turned back after a couple of steps. "Price, if the cops come after you, if they slap anything on you, call a lawyer and then call me, please. We have the death penalty in Oregon, this case isn't a joke. If you need any help or have any more questions about anyone else in the neighborhood, just give me a call. I'll do what I can to help, okay?"

I hugged the huge box of food to my chest and nodded as the vet disappeared around the corner, barely managing to throw the box onto the hood of Agatha's car before I spewed two large matcha soy lattes down the drain.

CHAPTER TWENTY-ONE

"WOW, YOU LOOK LIKE A SACK OF DOG SHIT." AGATHA sniffed the air around my face. "And you smell like coffee-flavored vomit."

I was too tired to respond and simply dropped the keys next to the door and hauled the box of take-out into the living room. "Where are the guys?" I looked down to see three cats sprawled on the floor, sleeping. They were cats and they were sleeping. Disappointment hit me like a sucker-punch, and I felt my jaw tighten as Agatha danced around me, her beady eyes fixed on my face. I dropped the food on the table with a thud. "Whatever. Like I give a rat's ass."

Fighting tears of frustration, I slipped out of the apartment and made my way down to the thrift shop. I sat in the large velvet chair for a long while, staring at the wall and trying to remember when I'd last been truly happy. A jumble of images from the past few days filled my mind and I grabbed a satin cushion and pressed it against my face. Happiness inspired by people who were half-cat didn't count, right? I groaned into the pillow. Maybe I had been happy when I opened my juice bar? But I knew I hadn't been, not really. Not when I remembered Gerard's patronizing pep talks or the way he scowled when he checked my accounts at month-end. And it wasn't when Gerard asked me to marry him, offering me the ring with one hand and taking my life-savings with the other. But I hadn't minded giving him my money, because he needed it. For the yogalates business. Our business.

"No, Price, you silly, silly woman. His business," I muttered. I lifted the pillow and flung it as hard as I could at the huge mirror on the far wall.

Agatha appeared around the corner. "What seems to be the trouble, hipster?"

I glared at her, waiting for a sarcastic remark, or a sly dig about my harem, but it never came. I sank back into the soft velvet and stared at the ceiling. "Everything. Everything is wrong. I need a damn fresh start, but I've just jumped from the frying pan into the fire, and I have no idea how to fix it." I opened my eyes and stared at the old witch. "I've been running in circles all day, and I still have no answers. Or maybe too many answers. Are you sure there's absolutely nothing that you remember surrounding your death, Agatha?"

The old woman scrunched her face and frowned, her shoulders sinking slightly as she came closer toward me. "I'm sorry, but there's nothing. Whenever I try to remember, it's as if my entire mind goes fuzzy. It's just blackness, and everything around it is mist."

I rubbed my eyes, exhaustion setting in deep within me. I leaned back in the chair and pressed my cheek against the smooth velvet. "Frankie. Harlow. Who else? Who else could there be? Surely, there must be something that I've missed. Somebody with a better motive than a failed fashion blog or rumored loan sharks, right?" Agatha didn't respond and irritation turned to fury in my aching gut. "Come on, Agatha, you've got to remember something. This is all your fault, damn it. If you hadn't left me the house, nobody would care about me. The cops would leave me alone. Why did you do it?" I glared at the ghost. "Why leave this place to me? I'm nobody. You never even met me. We never even did a proper interview."

"I was looking for someone special," Agatha finally whispered. I opened my eyes and met her gaze, her baby blues as clouds before a rainstorm. "I remember I needed someone specific. Someone important." She crossed over to me and brushed my hair off my face with feather-light strokes. Then she plucked a beautiful jeweled barrette from a shelf and slid it into my hair. She smiled. "A gift from a witch to keep you safe, dear." Her form began to shimmer and fade, but her words remained long after she vanished. "You must be something special for me to leave it all to you, of that I'm sure."

"Somebody special," I whispered. "Some special sort of fool." But I wasn't a quitter. I clenched my teeth, dragged my sorry ass out of the chair, and set myself to work. Settling in behind the dusty computer in the back corner office, I began searching through every possible person, place, event, or whatever I could think of that could possibly be related to Agatha's death. After two fruitless hours of frustration, I sat back and stared dry-eyed out into the silent thrift shop. The fading sun cast a dusty glow and the atmosphere was eerie as I imagined scenes of the woman's death. Where exactly did it happen? Scanning the large cluttered space, I shivered as I pictured her lifeless form on the floor. Shaking the images from my head, I leaned back in the chair and let out an exasperated groan.

"No luck?" A deep male voice sounded from within the shop. I recognized it as Tom's and turned my attention back to the computer.

"That's an understatement," I replied, preferring the frustration of my failed research to the inevitable condescension that was coming my way. "Look, I'm doing my best to figure this shit out. I don't need anyone to give me a hard time about it, okay? I've had a rough day."

The large black cat appeared next to me, his scruffy

fur and bulky build nearly as intimidating as his human form. I glared down at him as he sauntered up to me and rubbed up against my leg. I barely had time to react before the large tattooed naked man stood beside me, his full frontal nudity in all its massively embarrassing glory exposed perfectly at eye height from my chair.

"Zinging zucchinis," I cursed, shielding my eyes. "Put that thing away. You guys really need to get a handle on this whole shifting thing."

Tom reached for a flannel sweater that hung on a near rack, wrapping it around his middle for at least a somewhat false sense of modesty. "Better?"

I opened my eye to peek and nodded slowly. "I guess. What are you doing down here?"

Tom picked up a magazine from one of the vintage stacks near the desk and flipped through it for a long, drawn-out minute before turning his attention back to me. I tried to return my focus to the computer screen but my gaze was drawn to the half-naked man as if his skin was magnetic. My eyes traced the path of his Celtic tattoo from his neck, down his back and around his side where it wound lower, deep into the V of his hip. I glanced up from the shaded muscle just above his crotch to find him watching my face with slightly parted lips. I steeled myself for a mocking comment about whether or not I would like to a closer look, but unlike Pussy, Tom said nothing. He just stared at me with lips so soft I wondered how they'd feel on my skin.

"Thought you could use some company," he finally replied as he let his eyes fall on a spread in what I read to be '*Volume 7 - Women's Fashion of the 1930's*'.

"Oh," I said. "Thank you."

"You sound surprised." He gave me a probing stare and I turned away, embarrassed. "Is there anything I can help with?"

"I don't know. Maybe? I'm trying to dig up information on Agatha and her friends and family, but apart from the odd social media page, I'm coming up dry. I ran a juice bar, for heaven's sake, I'm not a journalist. I don't know how to investigate people." I glowered at the computer screen as if it owed me answers.

"Hey, don't be so hard on yourself, Price. You're doing a better job than that bastard Bert is," Tom replied, tugging on a second sweater he found lying nearby. I caught a glimpse of round, firm buttocks as he twisted to adjust the sweater covering his nether regions and my fingers itched to pinch his warm flesh. I stared down at my hands, mortified by my uncharacteristic thoughts. Tom stepped closer to me and I forced myself to focus on his face. "The fact that the cops seem so interested in you proves how incompetent they are, doesn't it?"

"Not really," I replied, though I appreciated him trying to make me feel better about the whole mess. "I came into the picture out of nowhere and inherited everything Agatha owns. If I were investigating a suspicious murder, I would be the first person I would suspect."

"You're obviously not the one who did anything, though," he replied.

I huffed out a frustration-filled groan. "I know that. We know that. But I have no way of proving it."

"So, I repeat," he said. "Is there anything I can help with?"

I turned off the computer, resigned to the fact that I wasn't going to get any further online. I thought back on the conversations I'd had over the past few days, and whether there was anything I was missing. "It would help to know more about you guys and this house."

"Okay." Tom rested his back against the wall, bare ass pressed against the plasterboard, and raised his chin. "What would you like to know?"

I shrugged. "Anything, really. I've been here a few days now and I still know nothing about you guys and why you're here. How you're here, really. I've just sort of accepted this as my own alternate version of reality because Agatha says familiars don't remember their previous lives, but you're not really familiars anymore, right? At least not full-time. Do you remember anything yet? How did you come to be here as a cat? Were you a cat first? A human first? I can't believe I'm actually asking these questions." I dragged my hands through my hair, hysteria building again like it had in the parking lot earlier that day. "Oh, my God, I'm losing it. I'm losing my grip on everything."

Tom leaned forward and placed his large hands on my shoulders, steadying me. The warmth he gave off comforted me and excited me both at the same time. I bit my lower lip and averted my gaze, embarrassed by the nearness of him. He responded to my withdrawal by leaning in even closer, pressing harder against my arms and holding me steady. "Slow down there, Price. One breath at a time. I know it's been overwhelming for you. I'll try to make sense of what I can for you, okay?"

"Okay," was all I managed to say, my voice catching in my throat.

"Let's start at the beginning," he murmured. "Not that it's much of a beginning. I don't know if it's the familiar spell, or this is just what I've always been, but I don't remember much of anything before this house, to be perfectly honest with you. It's all I know. And if I'm being perfectly truthful, I honestly don't remember ever being a guy before you showed up. So, maybe I was a cat first? But that doesn't seem right. It feels so natural to be human." He then paused and looked off into the far corner of the room, his own eyes turning haunted. "You know what? I guess I never really thought of it before. Sort of like you said, you just accept it as your own weird version of reality."

My chest ached. "So you don't actually know who you are? Or what you are?"

"No, I don't." Tom's hands were still on my shoulders, his body so close that I could feel the heat radiating from his skin. "All I know is that since you woke us from that spell, my whole world seems to be wrapped around this house." His eyes met mine. "Around you. And I don't know how I'm supposed to fix this mess for you, Price. I don't have a damn clue what I should do to make you feel better." I didn't move, didn't dare to breathe in case he could see the thoughts sliding through my mind. His voice was rough as he leaned into me, his mouth inches from my lips. "Tell me what I can do to make the pain go away."

My breath was ragged. "I don't know," I lied. "I don't know how you could make it better."

"I do," a voice purred. I jumped out of Tom's grasp, flustered, and stared as Muffin rubbed against my leg and popped back into human form, having the grace to turn the other way and conceal his manly bits from me as he shifted.

"You know how to fix the shit-show that is Pricetag's life?" Pussy drawled, sauntering into the room. "And what exactly would that be, genius?" The tabby cat rubbed himself against my leg, continuing to stroke my skin for a moment too long after he had returned to human form. I jerked my leg away and shot him a warning look, but he simply stood up slowly and stretched his hands over his head, naked as the day he was born and far, far happier. Tom grabbed a robe from a rail and threw it at Pussy, who slid his arms into the sleeves and tied the robe so loosely that I doubted it would conceal any of his essentials for very long. Pussy turned toward Finn again and cocked an eyebrow. "Well, enlighten us. How are we going to solve the problems of the world?"

Finn spun on his heels and pulled two rather large bottles of liquor from the cabinet on the wall behind me. "Easy. We get drunk."

CHAPTER TWENTY-TWO

"YOU KNOW WHAT, YOU GUYS?" I DRAWLED, MY WORDS slurring through my lips as I spoke. "This is the best idea anyone's ever had." I tumbled slightly and Finn had to catch me as I nearly fell over onto my face. We both doubled over laughing, inebriated beyond words. Two empty whiskey bottles rolled around the ground, not a drop left.

The three guys had put on the most ridiculous of outfits, collected from an assortment of strange attire found throughout the thrift shop. Tom had put music on, and the four of us ran around like idiots, prancing among the displays, not even caring if any of the passersby on the sidewalk could see in. It felt incredibly freeing; exactly what I needed after a very stressful few days.

"Oh, oh, oh," I practically yelled, my voice an

octave higher than usual. "Board games! Let's play a board game."

Finn gasped and clapped his hands together like a child. "Yes! I love board games. Let's see what we can find. There's got to be some around here somewhere."

The four of us rummaged through the thrift shop for a few minutes before Tom shouted his success from the far corner. "Found one! Vintage *Star Trek* Monopoly, how does that sound?"

I fell to my knees laughing when he brought out the massive box with a faded graphic on top. I raised my eyebrows up with both fingers and mocked a stern expression. "Okay, but I get to play as Spock."

"Fine, but dibbs on Luke Skywalker," Finn yelled, grabbing the box from Tom's hand and lifting the lid off of it to peer inside.

Rolling his eyes, Pussy pushed him aside, pulling the box into his own hands. "That's Star Wars, you idiot. Wrong franchise." He shuffled his fingers through the box and smiled up at me, shrugging in defeat. "Looks like everything is here. Shall we make this a drinking game?"

Still on the floor, I reached for both bottles and lifted them in the air, an exaggerated pout on my lips. "No more liquor."

"Surely there has got to be more somewhere," Finn said, running across the shop to the back where the cabinet was. A few loud crashes and bangs sounded from the back room, but he came out looking defeated. “Nothing. What the hell? Agatha drank like a fish, you would think she’d have far more than just two bottles of booze around here.”

Brow furrowed, Tom grunted. “I bet she’s hiding them. Seems like something she would do.”

I rolled my eyes and awkwardly pushed myself to a standing position, using a display case for support. “Oh, I know,” I gasped, my hands in the air and my fingers pointing around rapidly like little dancing guns. “Let’s go dancing. I love to dance. Can we go dancing? Pretty please?”

I gave the three guys my best doe-eyed expression. I even batted my eyelashes like a proper princess.

“I don’t see why not,” Tom shrugged. He pointed his finger at me. “But I’m there for the drinking, not the dancing, got it? Under no circumstances will you find me on that dance floor.”

I grinned, swaying slightly. “Sure thing, my fluffy-wuffy friend.”

Finn lifted one shoulder and glanced at Pussy. “It would be nice to get out of the house for once, right?”

Pussy met his eye for a moment before a slow smile spread across his handsome face. “Why the hell not? I haven’t been in a bar in years. I think?” Pussy scratched his head and looked at the two other guys. “Years? Does that sound right? That sounds… odd. Honestly I have no idea. I’m too damn drunk.”

"Yeah!" I squealed. "Dancing. All right, awesome. Where should we go? Anywhere good around here?"

"We've been cats, Price," Tom said. "What would we know? Check online, there's sure to be a place close by."

A quick search on my phone through drunk, squinted eyes told me that there was an Irish pub just down the road. "Perfect, I love the Irish. Let's go."

Not bothering to change out of their ridiculous clothes, we all grabbed colorful jackets from the front display rack and sprang out of the thrift shop like four people on a mission.

The air was cool and felt good against my flushed skin. I was far drunker than I cared to admit. If Gerard had ever caught me this inebriated, he would have given me the cold shoulder for a week. I blew a raspberry in the air at the memory of my douchebag ex and announced, "I'm having a double vodka the minute we get there." I waved my hands, teetering on the edge of the curb. "No, no. I'm having a Sex on the Beach cocktail. With a whiskey chaser."

Pussy sidled up to me and caught me by the arm. He winked at Tom and Pussy. "Sex on the Thrift Shop floor with a chaser of three cats in your bed sounds like a better option."

I snickered, too far gone to chastise him. "Hey, I've had worse offers," I slurred.

Tom chuckled and linked my other arm. "Easy,

cowgirl. Let's nobody say anything they'll regret in the morning." He kept his eyes trained on the street in front of us, but his fingertips gently caressed the inside of my wrist.

I yelled at Finn to link onto Pussy. "Come on, Muffin, we're the Monkees. Remember that old show? Let's do the walk. We're so damn funny. Cats are a hoot." Tom and Finn exchanged a look over my head and laughter filled the street. Arm in arm, the four of us flew on down the sidewalk, practically skipping on our way to the pub. "I hope they have a live band," I mused. "I love dancing to live music."

Tom grumbled, "I don't care what's there, so long as they have whiskey. Lots of whiskey."

The pub was only a few blocks down the road, and we were there before I had a chance to even get cold. To my excitement, there was a live band in the back playing an assortment of chart-toppers and pub hits. I dragged the guys to the dance floor, bouncing between all the sweaty people in the pub, but Tom slithered out of my grip and headed toward the bar, shooting me a slow smile over his shoulder. I watched him go, butterflies dancing in my stomach. It was the whiskey—had to be the damn whiskey.

Strong hands caught me by the waist and spun me around. I twirled out of Pussy's arm and Finn grabbed hold of me, lifting me off the ground as if I was a tiny ballerina instead of a lanky athlete. The sensation of freedom swelled inside me and burst out of my mouth in a song as I howled along with the band, twirling and wiggling to the music. The three of us let loose and danced like idiots to the loud music. If there was a better feeling in the world, I hadn't felt it yet.

We danced for what seemed like hours, and all my worries melted away. The music slowed and the two men closed around me. Finn hooked his arm over my shoulder and Pussy's hand slid around my waist. Eyes closed and arms raised, we swayed to the ballad, completely lost in the sounds of the lead singer's accented vocals. He really did sound Irish as he crooned about his lost lover on the other side of the ocean. When the song ended, the feeling of warmth and security surrounding me melted away, and I opened my eyes with a start.

"Finn?" I screwed my eyes up, scanning the thick crowd. "Pussy?" A cute guy with a goatee gave me an appreciative once-over and reached for my body. I slapped his hand away. "Ew, no. That wasn't an offer, I'm just looking for my friend Pussy." The man made a face. I raised my arm over my head. "He's about this tall, and he's got this great blond hair, like somebody in a magazine." I leaned forward as if I was sharing a secret, the liquor in my veins causing me to stumble slightly. "And he's hot. So are his friends. Like, super-duper hot. Abs as hard as like steel, perfect butts, and big, huge—" I stopped short, my pulse suddenly racing as I caught sight of three full outfits of clothing scattered around the ground. “Oh shit.”

The stranger I’d been talking to reached for my hand and started to murmur about how I could check out how he measured up to my friends, but I pushed him away with a grimace. I shook my head as I turned away from him. Firstly, my friends had vanished; I had no time for a booty break. Secondly, I was pretty certain he wouldn’t measure up all that well to any of my three guys. “My harem.” I giggled to myself as I made my way unsteadily through the piles of clothing. “My reverse harem.”

I stared down at the discarded clothes and nudged them with my toes, reality suddenly piercing my drunken daze. Oh freak. Cats. The guys had turned into cats. In the middle of a pub. “Okay, this is why we can’t leave the damn house,” I muttered to myself as I frantically looked around the floor of the pub. People were jumping and dancing and acting just as big of idiots as we had been moments before. The poor three cats didn’t stand a chance under the feet of the dancing stampede.

Running to the far corner where it seemed quietest, I came upon the three of them huddled together. “Well, shit,” Tom snarled. “This is why we shouldn’t make stupid ass decisions when we drink.”

I shushed Tom loudly, standing in front of them to block their view as people started to notice the three cats in the pub. The few people around us stopped dancing and stared down at them, confused. I waved them away and said they'd escaped my house and I was coming to collect them. I reached for them, but Muffin hissed at me, claws outstretched.

"What the hell?" I demanded.

"Don't touch us, we'll turn back to human and we'll be naked in the middle of the damn pub," Pussy hissed. I glanced around and fortunately most of the people had turned their attention back to their own partying. I must've looked like a lunatic talking to three cats in the corner of a pub. But then again, I'd seen stranger things in bars.

"Okay, then, what the heck do you suggest we do?" I asked

"Meet us outside," Tom said. "Lead the way and we'll follow behind. We need to get back to the house."

I groaned and nodded, pushing my arms out to nudge the crowd aside as I made my way out to the front of the pub. People grunted and moaned angrily at me as I shoved them to one side, but I sprang forward at a fast pace, glancing down constantly to make sure the three cats were close behind.

I barely made it to the front door, when someone caught my eye. I froze, my blood running cold. Standing at the far wall, leaning against the sidebar, was Officer Bert Fitzgerald. His face was pulled tight in an expression of annoyance and his lips curved down in a deep, disapproving frown. His eyes caught mine, and we stared at each other for a long moment. For a split second, I had the drunken urge to run up and smack him in that chubby little face of his for the stress he had caused me. But then I stopped and considered the ramifications that would cause me. I turned on my heels and bolted straight to the front door, hoping he wouldn't follow me.

When we finally made it out of the pub, to the ever confused expressions of the patrons and bartender at the front bar, we ran a few blocks down the road and turned down an alley, stopping only when I was sure we were out of sight from anyone standing outside the pub. When I peeked around the corner and saw that Officer Bert hadn't followed, I leaned against the rough brick wall of a commercial building, allowing my head to fall back against the rough cold surface as my heartbeat returned to its usual rhythm.

"What the hell? We didn't need to run that far," Pussy's voice panted up to me. "Your legs are much longer than ours, remember."

"Officer Bert," I huffed, my breath coming in gasps.

Tom's voice was filled with concern. "What?"

"Officer Bert. Inside the pub. He was there, he saw me." Panic filled me again, and I began hyperventilating.

"Okay, it's fine," Finn said. "I mean, it's a shame he saw you drunk, and weird that he saw you with three cats, but he didn't follow us. We are good, don't worry. It's not as if he can arrest you for being a drunken mess." Finn paused. "Well not in a pub while he's off duty, anyways. Let's just get home and put you to bed, how does that sound?"

I nodded my agreement, and we slowly made our way home, staggering intoxicated, laughing and nearly crying the whole way, using the back alleys and finally entering the house through the back door. I was drunk and exhausted and overwhelmed, and I could feel myself shivering. I wasn't sure if it was from the cold, the liquor, the adrenaline, or the seed of fear seeing Officer Fitzgerald had sown in my gut.

"Well, well. Somebody looks like they had a fun time," Agatha's voice drawled from the hallway as we entered.

I loosed a breath and walked her past her. I was too damn tired to bicker. "It's been a long day, Agatha. I'm going to bed."

"Your hair looks pretty," she said to me.

I paused and turned back to her, my expression shocked. Did she just pay me a compliment? Where did that come from? I stared at her for a long moment, frowning. "You look nice, too." I awkwardly blurted out, unsure really how to respond. Not that her appearance changed at all, anyways, considering she seemed to be stuck in one form as a ghost.

She smiled at me and waved me away, and I pretty

much crawled up the stairs into the bedroom and fell back semi-unconscious into the bed, not bothering to even get out of my clothes. The three cats joined me and sat on the side of the bed, looking up at me. I turned my head on the pillow, gazing down at them. "You want me to turn you all back?" My voice was ragged, exhaustion filling me as my eyes slowly closed.

"No, I think you need some extra special cat comfort tonight," Finn said.

"You mind if we curl up at your feet?" Tom asked, his voice soft.

My lips tugged up into a smile, as I snuggled into the comforter, pulling it tightly around me and patting the top of it for the three cats to jump up. "Stay on top of the comforters, okay? No surprise male nakedness."

I felt the three of them jump up on the bed and snuggle in around me. Just as I sunk into a deep, dreamless drunken sleep with the three strange house cats cuddled at my feet, I remembered something. My lips were almost too heavy to move them. "I never even got my Sex on the Beach."

Whatever reply Pussy gave was too muffled by the comforter to reach my ears, but the other two cats convulsed into fits of laughter, their warm bodies vibrating against my side like massage balls and lulling me into a deep, peaceful sleep.

CHAPTER TWENTY-THREE

I yawned and stretched, my body aching. Early morning light flooded through the window onto my bed and warmed my skin. My hangover was tremendous and my head pounded in a fascinatingly painful rhythm against my pillow. I rolled over, but found myself stuck. My comforters were pinned down. Inching onto my side, I slowly opened my eyes and nearly let out a scream.

Snuggled beside me were three rather large, rather unnervingly sexy naked men. "Out," I demanded, nudging them with my feet. "This wasn't our agreement. Out, all of you."

"What?" Finn yawned as he stretched. He looked around and had the grace to blush when he caught sight of the tangle of naked bodies sprawled over my legs.

"Shit, sorry. I must have touched off you in my sleep. Totally accidental, I swear."

Pussy opened his eyes lazily and stretched his long, toned body with a grin. "Speak for yourself, Muffin." I lifted my knee in an attempt to knock him off the bed, but he merely rolled onto his stomach so that his bare buttocks were facing the ceiling and his morning glory was pressed into the comforter beside my leg. I shot him a dirty look and wriggled away, fighting the temptation to land a smack on his naked butt. It would be satisfying to hear my palm slap down on those firm globes, but I was pretty certain I'd get more than I bargained for if I started that nonsense. Pussy's eyes were on my face and his lips curved as if he could read my mind. He ran a hand through his messy blond hair. "Don't be so grouchy, Pricetag. Unless you're still upset about not getting that Sex on the—"

Tom shouldered Pussy clear off the bed with a single jerk of his tattooed body, and Pussy stared up at us from the floor with an indignant scowl and an impressive full-frontal display. I threw my hands up to cover my eyes. "Guys! You're killing me. I'll keep my eyes closed, just cover yourselves up and go, please." I opened my fingers a crack as the floorboards creaked, closing them again tightly when Tom glanced in my direction. A low rumble of laughter filled my ears. Damn it, caught red-handed. Before Tom could tell the others about my peeping tendencies, the sound of loud knocking echoed through the house.

"What the?" I squeezed my eyes shut as my temples throbbed. "Is that in my head or is somebody really banging on our door?" The sound came again, and all three men looked around confused. Okay, so it wasn't just me.

"Who the hell is that?" Tom scowled in the direction the noise was coming from.

"Are you guys expecting someone?" I asked, sitting up and tugging on the comforter to cover my bare chest. When had I taken my damn clothes off? I looked around the room and saw my clothes strewn across the floor. I must've gotten hot and peeled them off while I was in a drunken coma. I groaned and felt my blush deepen, wondering if the guys had witnessed the event.

"Of course we're not expecting anyone," Pussy sneered. "We're cats, remember?"

I slithered off the bed, trying my best to conceal my dignity. "You are people now, not cats, okay?" Tom and Finn had covered themselves with towels from my press, but Pussy was still butt naked, holding one of my shirts over his crotch. I stared at him pointedly. "Now, go put some proper clothes on and let me get dressed in privacy, please."

The three men left the room, Pussy's bare ass a sight to behold in the morning sun.

Knock knock knock.

"Can someone get the door?" I yelled as I tugged my clothes onto my uncoordinated body. I stumbled around, still feeling the effects of the alcohol from the night before. I heard a few thumps and loud swearing coming from downstairs. I started toward the hallway. "Guys? What the hell is going on?"

Thunder sounded on the stairs as all three men ran back to the bedroom, only half dressed. "Price, something happened."

I grabbed hold of the door handle. "What are you talking about?"

Finn took a step forward with his hands outstretched like I was a wild animal that might bolt. "Don't panic, okay?" I glared at him, silent. "It's probably a big misunderstanding, but it looks like media is here." He paused. "On our doorstep."

"What?" It was too early for games. "Who the hell is Media?"

"Not Media," Tom growled. "The media. Someone called the media. The press. Newspapers, television. There are about forty journalists standing outside with cameras and microphones."

I hated alcohol; I was going to vomit. "Why are they here? Is this about Agatha?" Another thought hit my brain and I felt the blood drain from my face. "Oh, my God, they saw you turn into cats. They're going to try and take you away. Oh, my God."

Finn wrapped his arms around me as my shaky legs

began to buckle and pulled me onto his lap on the bed. "Take it easy, we're not going anywhere, Price. I swear." He brushed a tangled lock of dark hair off my cheek, his green eyes dark. "They're not here for us."

"No," Pussy agreed. His arms were crossed as he leaned back casually against the wall; only the tightness of his jaw and the straight line of his mouth gave away his worry. "From what I could hear through the door, they're here to investigate the girl who's suspected of murdering Agatha Bentley."

"What? That's insane. It's not fair," I insisted. "What would have brought them here? I'm not even an official suspect. I haven't even been brought to the station for questioning yet."

"Someone must've said something or leaked a rumor to one of the agencies." Tom's voice was like sandpaper and his hands were curled into fists. "This is a damn dirty investigation, when I figure out who's trying to set you up…"

I slid off Finn's lap and brushed Tom's shoulder with my fingers. "Take it easy, Fluffy. We don't need you up for murder charges too, all right?" Tom's body relaxed under my touch and I gave him a half-smile. "Who'd be our resident grumpy bastard if you got locked up?" His teeth were strikingly white against his olive skin as he flashed me a grin. I bit my lip, turning back to the others. "Okay, no more time for dicking around, we need to figure out who the fudge is trying to cover their dirt by flinging it at me."

Finn nodded, fumbling in Agatha's bedside locker and retrieving a notepad and pen. "Okay, who's our number one suspect? It has to be somebody with a reason to murder Agatha and then means or the influence to cover it up."

"Right." I sat down on the bed beside him and crushed my hands between my knees. "Frankie has a motive; Agatha crushed his dream and threw him out on the street. And it wasn't the first time his life had been ripped apart. That stuff takes its toll on a person." I stared at my feet, trying to gather my thoughts. "And he has a direct line to the chief of police in the city."

"What?" Pussy asked, cocking an eyebrow. "The vet's assistant has influence over the chief of police?"

"Apparently so," I said. "Bianca D'Arcy told me yesterday that her dating agency had paired them up and apparently the chief is head over heels crazy about Frankie."

Tom pressed his knuckles against the wall. "Shit."

"Okay, that's a possibility." Finn scribbled something on the notepad before turning his green stare back on me. "What about Agatha's cousin, Harlow?"

I frowned. "Well, if what Bianca says about his debt problem is true, and if it's true that this place could be worth a lot when the property market changes, I guess he could have wanted Agatha dead for her inheritance."

I tucked my hair behind my ears. “He swore he knew Agatha wasn’t going to leave him anything in her will and he seemed pretty convincing, but—“

“If somebody has the balls to strangle an old lady in her own home, they probably have the balls to lie without cracking,” Pussy interjected.

I nodded. “Pretty much. And Bianca insinuated it wasn’t the first time he’d been on the wrong side of the law.”

“Bianca,” Tom muttered. I glanced at him. “Bianca, Bianca, Bianca. She’s really stirring the pot, isn’t she? Dropping all those interesting little hints in your ear. You know she’s one of the wealthiest women in Salem, right? If anyone could pull strings in City Hall, it’s her.”

Finn shook his head. “But why? She has all the money she could ever want.”

“And she wasn’t even in the country when Aggie died. She told me she was at a conference in San Francisco that week, addressing hundreds of dating experts every day. Pretty rock solid alibi,” I said.

The banging on the front door started again, increasing in intensity with every passing second. Tom began to pace the floor like a lion in a cage, anger flaring in his eyes. Every muscle in his bare torso strained against his inked skin as he clenched his fists. “Whoever the hell is behind this, I’m going to find them. I swear to God.”

I watched him pace back and forth, my stomach

flipping and my chest tightening. Did he really care that much about me? I reached for him and grabbed his hand, pulling him onto the bed beside Finn and me.

"I told you, getting angry won't solve anything, Tom." I slid my hand along the side of his arm and his muscles rippled under my fingers. My phone buzzed on the side table and I grabbed it, swallowing a curse as Officer Bert's name flash across the screen.

"Who is it?" Finn asked. When I didn't answer, he eased the phone from my grip. His creamy complexion paled to alabaster. "Oh shit, Price, don't answer."

"You think he knows that the media is outside our house?" I asked, my mind spinning. I was definitely going to throw up.

"Of course he does," Pussy muttered. "The whole city will know before long. This kind of thing spreads quick, especially once it's in the news. Once you get the media involved, a frenzy always follows. Price, if they peg you as the murderer, everything is going to change, you do realize? That's how these things work."

"You think I don't know that, Pussy? This isn't my fault. I didn't ask for any of this." I fell back on the bed and covered my eyes with my hands, breathing in, counting to three, and letting it out slowly through my mouth.

A shadow fell over my face as something stirred above me and I opened one eye to find Pussy staring down at me with his brows drawn together under his thatch of blond hair. There was no trace of his usual arrogance, his face stripped bare. "I'm sorry, I wasn't trying to blame you." His voice was quiet. Soft. I raised my eyebrows and he gave me a tentative smile. "I'm a jerk when I get scared, Pricetag. And I don't want to lose you. We've only just found you."

I pulled myself into a seated position and punched him gently in the stomach, feeling the silky smoothness of his tanned skin under my fingers. "Don't be stupid, Pussy. You're not a jerk when you're scared." I paused. "You're a jerk all the time."

"Funny, Pricetag, very funny." Pussy's voice was loaded with sarcasm but the haunted look had faded from his eyes. He walked across the room and leaned on the windowsill. "Okay, we need a plan." Pussy gave me a forceful glare. "Under no circumstances can you leave the house, Price. You stay here with us, so we can protect you."

I shook my head. "I can hide all I want, Pussy, but as soon as the police get a warrant for my arrest, there'll be nothing stopping them from coming through that door and forcing me to go with them."

Tom smacked his fist into a pillow. "That's not gonna happen. They have nothing on you."

"You look so sure of yourself," I said.

"I am," he replied. His eyes burned like crystal fire as he held my gaze, sending a shiver down my spine.

My phone buzzed again, this time a text message.

"I'm outside, Priscilla. Come to the door." It was from office Bert.

I stood and turned my phone toward the guys so they could read the message. Finn stared at the phone. "A text message? What the hell is this guy angling at? You can't just text a suspect. My dad's a cop and he would never…" Finn's voice faded away as we all stared at him, open-mouthed. He sat back down on the edge of the bed. "My dad is a cop." He looked at us, his eyes as full as a spring pasture. "I remember his face. He's a cop."

Without thinking, I leaned forward and wrapped my arms around his neck and he buried his face in my shoulder. I ran my fingers through his hair, overwhelmed by the depth of emotion I could feel in his embrace. What the hell had Agatha done to these men? What could they have done that warranted a life sentence in a cat's form? Maybe she was right, maybe they deserved it, but looking around the room, I just couldn't believe that. And there was only one way to unlock the door to Agatha's magic and her memories, and if I went down for her murder... I straightened my back and reluctantly eased myself out of Finn's warm embrace.

"I'm going down to meet Officer Fitzgerald." I held my hands up to silence their protests and lifted my jaw. "Stop! I know you want to protect me, and I appreciate that, but I want to protect you guys too. And you need to respect that. You need to put your faith in me." Even though my stinking ex hadn't ever been able to put an ounce of faith in me. I slammed down the memory of Gerard's curled lip when I told him I was going to need a little more money to keep my juice bar in business, and I clenched my fists. "If there's any way to make this right, I'll find it, guys. But it's my battle. You've got to trust me enough to let me fight it."

Finn released his hold on my hand, and I stroked one finger along his jaw. "We'll talk later, about your dad." Pussy nodded to me as I passed, his arms folded tightly across his chest, and his face uncharacteristically somber. As I reached the bedroom door, Tom broke away from the others and blocked my path. A storm raged in the blue waters of his eyes. I placed my hand on his chest and leaned in, pressing my forehead against him. "I have to at least go talk to him, Tom. You know I do. Hiding inside will just make me look even guiltier."

His breath was a groan in my ear as he relented and shifted his body to let me pass. My phone rang and I glanced at the screen. Officer Fitzgerald again. I steeled myself. "Hello?"

"Priscilla? It's Officer Bert Fitzgerald." His voice sounded hoarse and ragged through the phone, nearly as exhausted as I felt.

"I got your message, what do you want, Officer?" I didn't bother to try and cajole him, it was way too late for any of that.

"The media got wind of the case, Priscilla. Somebody leaked some of my private notes." His voice was tight with barely controlled rage. "I need you to let me inside, Ms. Jones." When I didn't answer, he pressed on. "You realize I can get a warrant and come in?"

I ground my teeth together. "Office Fitzgerald, does the Chief know you're texting a suspect and making repeat house calls without—."

"They know about the juice bar, Miss Jones." Officer Fitzgerald's voice was softer than I'd heard it before. Almost kind. I leaned my weight against the doorframe and dragged air in through my teeth. "Look, I know it probably doesn't seem like this, but I'm on your side, Price. Just let me in. I'm alone and waiting I'm at the back door."

I killed the call and ran down the back stairs, gesturing for the men to stay in my bedroom and ignoring their shouts for information. True to his word, Officer Fitzgerald was waiting in the alley. I opened the door to let him into the apartment, but he gestured toward the thrift store instead. He closed the door softly behind us and I made for the velvet chair, but he called me back. "It's better if we stay right here, Miss Jones. We can't be seen from this angle."

"Okay," I said. I walked back slowly, not certain I wanted to be alone with the cop in a place I couldn't be seen by anyone else. I stopped several feet away from him. "Why are you here, Officer?"

Officer Fitzgerald crossed his arms over his broad chest. "I've been a cop for a very long time, Miss Jones. I started my career in Portland and I gave twenty years hard service there; I've always prided myself on being a damn good cop. But a few years ago, in Portland, I came up against a number of cases… Well, let's just say the cases were solved, but maybe I felt we didn't put the right people behind bars. Maybe there were powerful people pulling strings from high up." He paused and looked me straight in the eye. "Maybe they were trying to conceal the fact that there supernatural elements at play."

I drew in a breath, choking on my own spit and collapsing into a fit of coughing. "I'm sorry, a supernatural element?" My eyes burned as I blinked away tears of shock. If I'd been expecting the portly officer to drop a bomb on me, it certainly wasn't that one.

Officer Fitzgerald's cheeks colored slightly. "Look, Miss Jones, I know how crazy that sounds, and I don't expect you to believe me, but I need you to know that these people, the ones evading the law and bending the police force to their will, they'll do whatever it takes to pin the blame on somebody else. Anybody else." He reached into his jacket and pulled out a thick wad of paper, folded in half, and handed it to me. I opened it and glanced at the first page before folding it over again.

I didn't need to read the words, I'd read the file a thousand times before.

The officer nodded to me as he reached for the door, turning back before he pulled it open. "I'm not saying you had anything to do with Agatha Bentley's murder, Miss Jones, all I'm telling you is that somebody made sure that file landed on my desk this morning. Somebody who very much wants me to know about your money problems and the skeletons in your closet."

I nodded, and he stared around the thrift shop. "Agatha Bentley died in this room, Miss Jones, and it was either somebody Mrs. Bentley knew so she didn't put up a struggle, or somebody who's able to use some serious voodoo to make it look that way. Somebody damn dangerous, so if you have anything you need to get in order before my superiors hand down the order to bring you in for questioning; any alibi you need to be corroborated, any people you can call, now's the time to do it."

I was still standing inside the thrift store when the back door banged shut and the three guys eased themselves into the space around me, waiting patiently for me to speak. I held the wad of paper out woodenly and let them take it from me. Even my voice was tired. "I think things might be even worse than we thought."

CHAPTER TWENTY-FOUR

"You did what?" Pussy's voice was raised higher than usual, his expression unreadable.

"You don't understand," I said slowly, letting out a deep breath. "It wasn't my fault, it was my dickhead ex-boyfriend. He had offered to set up my insurance, because he had done it already for his own business. He promised he had it set up two years before, so after the fire burned down my business and I put my claim in, well…"

Tom rubbed his eyes with his hands, letting out a disgruntled breath. "Let me get this straight." His body was unnaturally still. "Your ex set up your insurance policy in both your names and the next week your business burned down and you made an insurance claim against it. A business that hadn't turned a profit in the entire time it had been open. Is that right?"

I swallowed hard and nodded. The sinking feeling in my gut deepened. "Yes, but I had no idea Gerard had only just set up the insurance or that he'd requested a waiver on the waiting period before a claim could be made. I had believed it had been set up for years. I know how bad this looks, but I swear to God, I had no idea."

"No shit, this looks bad." Pussy dragged his fingers through his hair. "You buy insurance, and the next week your failing business burns to the ground and you set up a claim? Jesus, Price."

Finn grimaced. "And now Agatha leaves everything to you randomly, you show up a couple of weeks later, and she dies." He dropped into a crouch against the wall. "Shit, Price. That looks like a pretty bad coincidence."

"Did they prove it was arson?" Tom's low tone was as heavy as thunder.

I shook my head. "It wasn't arson, I swear to you, I would never do a thing like that. I loved that stupid juice bar, even if it never made me a dime. And I didn't even get to keep the stupid money from the claim, I gave it all to Gerard to cover the money he'd poured into the place before it went bust." I stared at my feet. "I barely had enough money to cover my bus fare to Salem. Who the hell is going to believe I wasn't desperate enough to get rid of Agatha?"

Tom grabbed the paper from Finn's hands and flicked to the last page. "Not you, Price." He stabbed a finger at Gerard's signature. "Him. Did he burn your business down? He's the one who got the money, he's the one whose name is on every damn piece of paper." I closed my eyes against his question, the same one that haunted me every night since the fire department had called my phone. But I couldn't answer it, because if I did, if I admitted he'd done something so vicious, I'd have to admit to myself that I'd wasted ten years of my life on a man who didn't give a shit about me. And I wasn't sure that was a truth I could come back from.

Finn crossed the room and grabbed Tom's shoulder, shooting him a warning look. "Let it go, man. It's not the time." He turned to me and cupped my face in his large hands. "Price, what else did Officer Fitzgerald say? Why did he give you this? Why not just take you in for questioning?"

I stared into his green eyes, my calm in the storm. "He said he was on my side. That he didn't believe I was guilty but somebody higher up was making it impossible to ignore me as a suspect." I frowned, remembering his bizarre story. "He sounded pretty crazy; he seemed to think he'd been involved in other cases where the wrong person was convicted just to hide some supernatural element." Pussy's head jerked up and Finn stared at Tom over my head. "What?" I looked around at the three men. "He's just a crackpot."

Pussy took a step forward. "Says the woman who lives with a witch and her three familiars."

"That's different," I argued. "He didn't even mention anything about ghosts or magic in this case and it's hardly like Agatha is pulling any ghostly strings. The woman spends her time giving unsuspecting pedestrians the middle-fingered salute and flashing her knickers at the delivery man." The three men didn't look convinced. I spread my arms wide. "Come on, guys, get real. I know Agatha fancies herself as some big bad witch, but she doesn't have any high-powered magical enemies. She's an old woman who owned a thrift shop and was practically a recluse."

Finn frowned. "That's not true." He looked at the other men for support and they nodded. "I mean, maybe for the last few months after she fell out with her doll-making friends, but she was hardly ever at home before that."

"She loved getting into her car and tearing around the country," Pussy agreed. He pressed a hand against his stomach and made a face. "She was such a bad driver."

Tom smirked. "The worst." His lips thinned. "She was pretty low the last few weeks. though. She kept trying to leave the house but she just… couldn't. She couldn't make herself walk out those doors. And then Frankie left." He shook his head. "She only started to come round again when she found out you'd accepted the job."

"Yeah," I muttered. "Another genius decision from

Price Jones." Something tickled my memory as I imagined a depressed Agatha, unable to leave the house no matter how much she wanted to. Officer Fitzgerald's words came back to me like a bad dream, somebody Agatha knew or somebody with serious voodoo. Magic. Somebody with magic. I stared at the guys. "Agatha would never have been so depressed that she would…" The three men gave me a puzzled glance and I pursed my lips. "Is there any chance Agatha could have used magic to end her own life?"

"What? No," Finn said. He glanced at the others. "Right?"

Tom looked slightly less convinced. He pressed his lips together. "Maybe we need to talk to Agatha about what you've uncovered so far." He raised his eyes to the ceiling and called, "Agatha?"

"Aggy?" Pussy joined in. "Agatha, we've got liquor…"

The ghost didn't appear. Finn pushed the door open. "Back when she was alive, when she would get stressed out, she would lock herself away for hours in her study doing her scrapbooking or whatever the hell it was she did with all those clippings of hers."

"Thanks, Finn," I murmured. I made my way up the stairs, shielding my eyes from flashes of the cameras that tried to snap photos through the front entryway. The guys had pulled the curtains closed, but the lights were still bright, and it made my stomach churn.

I knocked gently on Agatha's study door, but there was no reply. After waiting a few seconds, I knocked again and pushed open the door. "Oh, sorry, I didn't think you were in here," I quickly apologized, seeing Agatha's small frame bent down over something on the floor.

Agatha looked up at me. "No bother, I was just fussing with something. How are you doing, dearie?"

I let the door fall closed behind me and gazed down at the large box that she had before her. "You know, I've had better days." Like the days when the media didn't think I was a killer and I didn't have to ask a ghost had they committed suicide. I offered the old woman a smile before returning my attention back down to the numerous clippings that she had piled in the shoebox before she slipped it away in the drawer next to her, slamming it shut.

The guys followed me into the room, but Tom and Finn turned into cats immediately as they arrived. I frowned at them and then looked at Pussy, still in human form. Agatha stared at the cats for a long moment before murmuring, "The magic is fading."

I raised my eyebrows. "You remember your magic?"

Agatha shook her head softly and stared down at the cats, a deep frown setting on her face. "No, not really, just little bits and pieces." She screwed her eyes shut and a look of fierce concentration crossed her face. "But I remember the magic is fading." She paused and looked me straight in the eye. "We're losing control."

"We? What do you have to do with this?" I looked at Agatha and then at the cats. "Your magic, Agatha? Is that what keeps turning the guys back into cats? Will they be your familiars forever? Unless we can fix your memory?"

Agatha froze in place, averting her gaze from mine. She stared into the corner of the room. "We're losing control of the magic. That's all I know. It's just a glimpse, but I can see it. I can sense it. The chaos, it's growing."

I took a step toward her. "Agatha, could that be why you reached out to me? Why you needed an assistant, one you thought was a witch? Could that be why you left everything in my name, because you were losing control of something?" I took another step, lowering my voice. "Is that why you stopped leaving the house, Agatha? Is that why you were depressed?"

"What?" Agatha turned her beady glare on me.

I swallowed. "Before you died, you were depressed—"

"Not that, the other thing," she snapped.

"About not leaving the house?" I said. "You hadn't left the building for weeks, you couldn't leave, do you remember? The guys said you felt like you were trapped?"

With a low hiss, Agatha vanished before I could ask

her anything else. I called after her, but she didn't reply. I turned back to Pussy, who frowned at me and knelt down next to the other cats, running his hand through his hair. "She's upset. I haven't seen her look this upset in a long time. Maybe just leave her be, Price?"

"I don't want to upset her, Pussy, but we need answers and fast. There are people outside the door baying for my blood. I need to find something to help us figure this out." I turned my attention to the drawer where Agatha had shoved the box, trying my best to ignore the constant buzz of noise from outside the store. I yanked the drawer opened and pulled out the shoebox Agatha had hidden away. "What was she doing here all day?"

Pussy shrugged and leaned back against the wall. "I don't know, maybe scrapbooking or some shit like that."

I flipped through the newspaper clippings in the box. There must've been hundreds in there. Some were new, but most were old and brittle. I picked them up as carefully as I could. I flipped through the first few and paused when my eyes fell on an image of a younger Agatha with a tall, elegant Asian man. I gasped as I stared down at him, confused. "Oh, my God."

Pussy edged closer to me to peer at the paper in my hand. "Who's that?"

"This is Dr. Lee," I whispered. I couldn't believe what I was looking at. "Agatha knew Dr. Lee? She recognized when I was using his calming technique when I first got here, but she never told me she knew him. " I stared down at the image, wondering just how well she knew the man. Had this photo just been taken in passing? Were they close? I had so many more questions for her, I wished she would come back. "Oh, my God. She's so lucky." Pussy raised one eyebrow. I grimaced. "Well, except for the whole murder victim thing, obviously."

I held the piece of paper against my chest. Agatha knew Dr. Lee. I felt my lips curve. Maybe she wasn't such an awful old witch after all. I placed the newspaper cut-out beside me before continuing to flip through the rest. If I thought I was shocked when I saw the photo of Agatha and Dr. Lee, what my eyes fell upon next nearly stopped my heart.

"What the freakin' fruit loops!" I turned to Pussy and the two cats. "Guys, you all need to see this." I felt my heart skip a beat in my chest as my skin grew cold and clammy. The two cats rubbed against my hand and all three men were in human form again. I didn't even care that two of them were naked, I simply held the piece of paper up to them for them to see. By the expressions on their faces, they were just as shocked as I was.

"Is that you?" Finn asked, his eyes wide.

I pulled the paper back toward me and gazed down at it, nodding slowly. "Yeah, it is. Why the heck would

Agatha have a newspaper clipping of me from this long ago?"

Tom shrugged and took the paper from my hand. "Maybe she was doing some research on you before your interview?"

I stared down at it and considered, but then frowned. "This newspaper came out five years ago. She wouldn't have any way to get her hands on a paper copy recently. She's had this for a while." I didn't know what to make of it. No matter what way I twisted the pieces of Agatha's puzzle, they didn't add up to a clear picture, and I was beginning to suspect that I was more involved in all this than Agatha had initially let on. Or that she could remember, anyway. "What the hell is going on here, guys?"

Finn shook his head and rubbed my back with his hand, soothingly. "It's just a photo, Price. Maybe it doesn't mean anything."

"A photo of me from years before I'd ever heard of Agatha Bentley or her crazy thrift shop?" I spread my hands wide for emphasis.

Finn relented. "Okay, it's really weird, you're right. I don't know, maybe you have a bigger role to play in Agatha's life than you think. Maybe you really are a damn witch. Maybe Agatha has the hots for you and has been secretly stalking you for the past five years." He dropped to the floor beside me. "I don't know why she has it, Price, but I really don't think she knows either.

She's crazy, but she wants this mystery solved more than anyone."

I swallowed the lump in my throat and placed the picture of me down, my eyes failing to pull away from the image of my younger self. I sighed and forced myself to consider Finn's logic. It was an image from ages ago, one that had been in a paper that was distributed all over Oregon, and Agatha had a billion paper cuttings. Who knew why certain things took her fancy? It could be explained by a thousand different reasons.

Flipping through the rest of the papers, I had nearly given up hope of finding anything useful, when I came to a folded piece of yellowed parchment at the very bottom of the box. I lifted and carefully opened it, the paper brittle and thin, like an old archival newspaper that hadn't been properly cared for.

"What's that?" Tom asked, looking over my shoulder at the delicate paper. I shrugged as I opened it as carefully as I could, the corners crumbling in my fingers. I very, very slowly unfolded the paper.

"Wow," I breathed. "The newspaper dates back to 1895." I pointed toward the date in the far top corner. The image was faded and I lifted it up to the light and looked closer. The air froze in my lungs. "Oh my God."

Over my shoulder, I heard the sharp intake of Tom's breath as he realized what we were looking at. I held the paper out for Finn and Pussy to see, while I screamed for the ghost. "Agatha Bentley, get your ass in her now. It's important!"

Grumbling, Agatha swept through the wall. "What's wrong with you, girl?" She gave me a disapproving once-over. "I thought my last assistant was shrill, but only dogs can hear you when you shriek like that. You'll wake the dead."

She smiled smugly at her own joke, but her grin faded when I held the piece of paper in front of her face. "This is you, isn't it?" I demanded. I knew the answer already. I jabbed at the date on the clipping and glared at the old witch. "This is you in 1895, Agatha." My lips felt dry enough to crack as I slid my finger down the page and landed on the smiling faces of the two figures standing next to Agatha in the photograph. "And that's Bianca and Dot."

CHAPTER TWENTY-FIVE

My heart was beating so fast I felt like I was going to pass out. Seeing the craziness my life had descended into on the sepia pages of a centuries-old newspaper was too much. I gaped at the ghost. "Agatha, this image is dated 1895. How is that possible?"

The old woman opened her mouth, but her answer was interrupted by fresh banging at the door. I cursed the journalists under my breath and turned back to Agatha.

Bang, bang, bang.

Tom was the first to jump to his feet as the sound of heaving wood filled the air. A loud voice called through the door, "Priscilla Jones, we have a warrant for your arrest. You need to vacate the property immediately and accompany us to the station."

I froze, staring up at Agatha, pleading with my eyes. "Agatha. 1895. I need you to remember. What's going on? How is this possible? It's 2018."

Agatha floated before me, open-mouthed for a long second, before she gasped and landed on the floor.

Bang, bang, bang. We were running out of time.

Agatha stared at me with eyes like pools of midnight oil. "I remember."

Bang bang bang. It sounded as if they were trying to break the door down. Tom, Finn, and Pussy looked as though they were going to explode, and my pulse raced as my heart thundered in my chest. I pleaded with her. "Please, Agatha. Tell me."

"Price," Tom cut in. He grabbed my shoulder in a tight grip. "We need to leave. If they get in here, they're gonna take you away."

I squeezed his hand, but continued pleading with Agatha. "Please, Agatha. Please. I need you to remember. Just remember!"

Agatha's eyes opened so wide that I could see the whites surrounding her irises. Her voice was a sweet lilting breeze, a child's song, and I swore I could her hear the cracked playing of a clockwork music box. "*Once we were witches, one, two, three. Friends and sisters for all eternity. Don't betray your sister, you know that isn't nice.*" Her voice lowered to a vicious whisper and I leaned forward to hear her final words. "*Don't betray your sister, or you shall pay the price.*"

I fell backward as the witch threw herself at me with her hands as gnarled as claws. I screamed, preparing for her attack, but she passed straight through me and flung herself down the stairs, screaming like a banshee as she hurled herself through the front door at the cops who had almost succeeded in breaking the door from its hinges.

In a heartbeat, Tom had me in his arms like a football and ran us back toward the rear door. We had almost reached the far wall when he turned back into a cat, and I came slamming down on the wooden floorboards, hitting my head hard. I rolled onto my back and groaned. I looked at the massive black cat.

"Shit, I'm so sorry, Price," he swore.

The other two cats skidded into the hall and we gaped down the stairs at the front door as it heaved one last time, the hinges nearly bulging free.

I reached for the cats to turn them back into human form, but they jumped back from me. "No," Pussy shouted. "You go. We'll take care of them."

I was frantic. "Huh? No! What are you guys going to do? You're three cats and a ghost."

The three of them huffed up, their fur standing on end. Tom's voice was a low snarl. "Trust us, we've got claws and teeth, we can do some damage. We'll stall the cops. You go talk to Dot and Bianca. I told you that Bianca bitch was wrapped up in this somehow."

Before Tom could say another self-satisfied word,

the door smashed open and splinters flew everywhere. I gasped and sprinted back through the door, slamming it behind me as I jumped into the car. I went to turn it on and realized I didn't have the damn keys. I looked down and saw them sitting on the passenger seat next to me with a sticky note with a little heart sketched on it. I looked up to see Pussy watching me through a window. He winked before disappearing in a puff of white and brown fur.

Just as the engine roared to life and I accelerated down the alley, two cops, neither of them Bert, smashed through the back door. In my rearview mirror, I saw the three massive house cats jump on the cops, slicing them with sharp claws and preventing them from pursuing me. I swerved as I nearly choked on my own breath, my foot firmly on the accelerator. I didn't pause as I screeched onto the street, revving the engine to speed past the bloodthirsty rabble gathered at the front of the building.

As I flew through the streets of Salem, a wave of emotions flooded through me. Panic, fear, but mostly guilt at having left the cats alone with people capable of hurting them. People armed with guns. What if they were taken by animal control? I nearly slammed on the brakes to turn around and go back to them, but the thought of Tom's face if I dared to come back without answers was enough to keep my car pointed in the right direction. I had to get the answers we needed. That was the only way forward. Answers, and then I would run back to them and this whole thing would just go away.

At least, that's what I told myself.

CHAPTER TWENTY-SIX

RETRACING MY STEPS FROM EARLIER, I MADE MY WAY back to Bianca's house with break-neck speed. My body shook, and my hands barely gripped the wheel as I tried to focus on traffic, weaving in and out of cars as I sped toward her large Art Deco home.

When I reached the gates, I pulled the car over, hardly bothering to park in line, and bolted up to her front entryway. After banging on her door for at least a few minutes, I figured she wasn't home, and ran back to the car and made my way to the only other place I thought she could possibly be. Arriving at Dot's bakery, relief filled me as my eyes fell on the two of them sitting sipping tea at the front seats of the bakery through the storefront window. On silent feet, I slipped inside.

"Price," Dot's cheerful voice chirped up at me as I

padded toward their table. A flush crept up on her cheeks as she lifted her tea to cover her mouth. "Lovely to see you here, sweetheart. Are you here for some more treats?"

I shook my head and pulled up a chair, sitting between the two. Dot smiled at me warmly. Bianca, on the other hand, wore an expression of pure steel.

"To what do we owe this pleasure?" Bianca asked, and from her tone I knew it was no pleasure at all.

"I know what you are," I spat. "I know you're witches." I folded my arms over my chest and glowered at Bianca. "And I'm pretty certain one of you is a very wicked witch."

Bianca stood up, and with a wave of her hand, everyone in the bakery vanished, the doors slammed shut, the lights dimmed, and the curtains closed. I wanted to clap my hands in delight, it was like a scene straight out of a wizarding movie, but I refused to give Bianca D'Arcy the satisfaction of my awe. I kept my lips pressed together tightly.

Bianca sat down slowly, her movements calculated. She turned her head in my direction in a fluid motion. *Exorcist*, eat your heart out. "Go on, Priscilla. You have our attention."

I leaned forward in my chair, feigning a confidence I didn't feel. "You know, when you told me you'd met Agatha working at the woolen mill, I hadn't expected it to be in 1895."

Bianca's pupils expanded and contracted like a nuclear explosion in her otherwise frozen face and I felt a kick of satisfaction in my gut. Take that, sly bitch. Dot reached for a piece of cake, stuffing it into her mouth with her fingers. I stared at the plump old woman as she avoided my eyes and opened my mouth to ask her something.

"Agatha was a special breed of witch, you could say." Bianca cut across me before I could address Dot and her steely voice sent a chill up my spine. She reminded me of Cruella Deville, with her over-the-top black fur coat and perfectly coiffed icy hair. "She was powerful, we sensed that the moment we met her. Dorothy and I had been raised in witching families, magic was part of our culture as well as our blood, but Agatha's mother was a Blank. A child with no magical ability, born into a witching family. She left the family home at a young age, met a man, had Agatha. When she realized what Agatha was…" Bianca's voice faltered and she frowned at the table for a moment before she spoke again. "Agatha bore the brunt of her mother's bitterness at being a Blank. The more Agatha's magical ability flourished, the more her mother made her suffer."

Dot took over the story. Her voice was strained. "By the time Sissy, Agatha's aunt, found her, Agatha had developed her own brand of magic, unbound by the rules and traditions those of us who grow up in magical families believe to be sacrosanct. Maybe it was in her nature, or maybe it was a result of her desperate need to find strength deep within herself to survive the terrible things she'd faced, but whatever the reason, by the time we met Agatha when she started working for my father at the mill, she was more powerful than any other witch I'd ever met."

"And we were drawn to her like moths to a flame, weren't we, Dotty?" Bianca's face softened as she looked at her old friend.

Dot chuckled and patted my hand. "We got into some scrapes in those first few years, I can tell you that much, Price. Damn near broke my parents' hearts. We went against all tradition and decided we weren't being sent off to some coven our parents chose; Portland or Newport or Astoria. Salem was a young city back then, with a very small magical population, and the witching council had no intention of granting the city rights to its own coven."

"But Agatha never needed permission from anyone to do a damn thing," Bianca said. The two smiled at each other, swallowed by their memories. Bianca's smile faded. "Then the flu came and it changed everything."

Dot nodded her head solemnly. "It was like the beginning of the end, that cursed flu." The old woman turned her plump face toward me. "Witching families are generally long-lived. Not immortal, you understand, but in good health, a witch could live for two hundred years. Maybe more. There aren't many witching families outside of the older cities and towns in the world, but they had survived well enough through the millennia. Until the influenza epidemic scoured the Earth."

"For whatever reason, witches were even more vulnerable than regular humans to the virus," Bianca said, taking over from her friend. "It ravaged the international witching community, and Agatha, Dot, and I all left Salem to help to rebuild the magical world. I ended up in Moscow, Dorothy in London, and Agatha in New York. We swore to each other we'd return to Salem and rekindle our little coven, but the flu was only the start of those dark days."

"The Great War, the Russian Civil War, the Depression, the Second World War," Dot said.

Bianca drew her perfectly groomed brows together. "The Cold War, Korea, Vietnam." She shook her head. "The darkness just kept coming and the magical community did their best, as they've always done, to fight that wickedness and to heal the broken."

"Witches can heal people?" The words burst from my lips before I could swallow them; so much for cool and disinterested.

Bianca cast a cold eye over me. "Witches do a great many things that the world will never know about. And we take great pains to ensure it stays that way." I shifted back in my chair, suddenly remembering what had brought me here. Bianca continued. "But a few decades ago, when we each reached our hundredth birthday, we were released from our duties and, one by one, we all drifted back to Salem and began to build our lives here again. Our second lives, as we witches call it, when our duty is done and our time is our own. And a second life is a very precious thing, Priscilla."

Dot patted my hand as Bianca shot me an ice-cold glare. Dot's voice was gentle. "It takes a lot of magic to allow a witch stay in the same city for their second life. Without the magic, people would begin to notice that we barely age. And every coven guards their magic very closely. Any change in the coven effects not only our own personal spells, but the entire coven's spells."

"Not that Agatha gave a rat's ass," Bianca hissed. "Oh no, Agatha had certain ideas about how things ran, and because she was powerful, she thought she could enforce those ideas on the rest of the coven—Dot and me."

Dot turned her big eyes on me. "It's true. She put us all at risk. We had no choice but to banish her to her home, else risk everything."

"Banish her?" I squinted at Dot, feeling as though I was suddenly five steps behind.

"Agatha wanted to change the coven, Price. Something has been happening to our magic, and she had a wild notion that she just needed to find the right witch and everything would be okay again." Dot's face was pleading. "She was acting crazy, saying she'd been searching for suitable candidates. Prowling orphanages, scouring homeless shelters—it was madness. We couldn't trust a stranger with all the magic tied to our coven. All our spells, all our secrets..." Dot's words faded into an anguished silence.

"Agatha was looking for someone and you didn't want her to find them," I said. "Because you wanted to protect your coven." It made sense in a weird sort of strange witchy way, but it hardly seemed real life. Although, given the strangeness of the last few days, I was willing to accept nearly anything at this point. I turned my head to stare at Bianca. "And to protect your coven, you paid somebody to strangle her to death while you had the perfect alibi of speaking at your fancy-pants conference, and then used your magic to distract the cops and point the investigation in my direction."

Dot let out a strangled yelp and Bianca stared at me a long moment before she frowned, her porcelain skin creasing as her lips curved into a frown and her eyes narrowed. "No, absolutely not."

I smacked my hands down on the table. "Bullshit."

Bianca's eyes blazed as she leaned over the table. "Watch your tongue, girl. You're on very shaky ground." She sat back, the rage smoothed from her face, and she folded her hands together in a steeple. "Yes, we fell out with Agatha, and yes, we did act against her."

"I knew it," I spat.

"You don't know anything, let me speak," Bianca snapped. "We worked a binding spell so that Agatha would be unable to leave her home and continue her search for a new coven member."

I stared from Bianca to Dot, who stuffed another piece of cake into her mouth. "That's why she became a recluse," I said. "You did that to her. You turned her home into a prison." I dragged my hands through my hair. "God, what a horrible thing to do. Did she know it was you? Did she know what was happening?"

Bianca raised her chin defiantly. "We wove a memory theft spell into the binding. If she guessed it was us, she'd forget the very thought even as it formed in her mind." I opened my mouth to express my disgust, but Bianca cut me off and pushed herself into standing position, glaring down at me, and I swear I could feel the air buzz with an electricity I hadn't felt before. Her voice changed as she spoke, and her words echoed through my head. "We didn't murder Agatha. I wasn't even here on the day of Agatha's death."

I returned her glare, refusing to be deterred. "You're a witch with a very healthy bank account. Maybe you hired somebody to kill her. Maybe you used magic to do it?"

Dot's chubby fingers scrabbled at the last crumbs as Bianca hissed at me. "Ignorant human. If I used my magic to murder Agatha, I'd be dead myself. Any witch who breaks the law of life by intentionally doing harm to their coven sister will face the same fate themselves. Do you understand, child? If I had a willing hand in Agatha's murder, I'd be a corpse."

Bianca stared at me with such ferocity that I dropped my gaze to the plate in front of me, following the line of Dot's body over her fingers and up her arm onto her ghostly pale face. The memory of her words when she gave me the apron she'd made for Agatha crawled over my brain like I spider. I answered without taking my eyes off Dot's face. "I do, Bianca. You're right. I had it all wrong. You didn't murder Agatha." I sensed her body relaxing from across the table, only to snap back to attention when I continued speaking. "You didn't kill Agatha, Bianca. Because Dot did."

CHAPTER TWENTY-SEVEN

"I'M SO SORRY," DOT WHISPERED, HER HANDS FINALLY still, releasing the crumbs trapped between her fingertips. Bianca's face was paler than a new moon as she tried to hush Dot, but the old woman silenced her with a wave of her plump hand. "No, Bianca. No more. No more lies, no more forcing people to do what we want. I can't live like that, by the wind and the water, I can't." She turned back to me. "I know you'll find this hard to believe, Price, but I thought I was helping."

"Helping?" I repeated. There was barely a sound from the street outside, except for the distant whining of a siren.

Dot nodded, glancing at Bianca. "Like we told you earlier, our magic is failing, dear. A witch draws her power from the leylines, but in order to tap into those lines, the magic of the blood must also remain strong.

It's like a teeter-totter, it there has to be a balance. Mother Nature will only grant a coven as much magic as their family blood can control. That's how it's always been, magic is passed down along bloodlines and new life is what keeps a family's magic strong; future generations to connect to the leylines and hold the balance."

I sat forward as understanding hit me like a fork of lightning. "Nobody in your coven has any children."

"No, dear, we don't." Dot's voice was heavy with the pain of a wound so deep it could never truly heal. A pain I'd watched from afar since I was a tiny child, the wound my mother carried like a knife in her back even after she adopted me. I filled the hole in her life, but never quite to the brim. I swallowed as Dot continued. "Bianca and I were content with our fate. We accepted the magic in our small coven would wane, but Agatha was never one to follow the rules. She was convinced she could game the system and find the right person to bolster our powers. But we knew it would just be trouble. If she found the wrong person, the ramifications could have been terrible. Our magic was becoming unpredictable as it was, can you imagine if we passed the magic to someone not in our bloodlines? The whole city could've been destroyed."

"Or worse," Bianca snapped. "Our magic could have been taken away completely."

I raised an eyebrow. Okay. Priorities, lady. Jeez. The

sounds of sirens grew louder as Dot continued speaking. "I agreed with Bianca that we had no choice but to banish her to her own home, so she couldn't search anyone out. I thought it was the right thing to do. I thought I could live with it." She lifted her eyes to look at her coven sister. "But I couldn't, Bianca. I couldn't bear to see her at that window, staring out at life from the prison we'd made for her."

Bianca was as stone-faced as granite as she listened to Dot, but the other woman didn't stop talking, her words flowing as though a dam had burst. "I waited until you had left the city and were far enough away not to feel my magic, and I cast a silencing spell to seal her lips from sharing any of our secrets." She turned her gaze to me, pain written on every feature. "It's not a dangerous spell, the person's lips are sealed physically for only a few minutes. I didn't even need to be in the building to work it, I stayed right here." She closed her eyes as if sorrow made it too hard to face the light. "It was a perfect storm of tiny mistakes. I guess Agatha was choking on that grape, right when I worked the spell."

I opened my mouth to ask about the marks on Agatha's neck, but Bianca answered for me, her voice as cold as ice as she stood from the table. "And when Agatha couldn't open her mouth to dislodge the grape, she tried to use magic to break the spell and ended up strangling herself with her own power."

"Bianca!" Dot called after her friend as Bianca

crossed the room with her phone pressed to her ear, raising her voice to be heard over the sirens in the street.

Reality hit me like a punch in the face as I stared at the flashing blue lights shining through the coffee shop curtains. I'd found the answers, but it didn't matter. How could I prove any of it? How could I defend myself when the truth was so much less believable than the fiction? Dot stared from me to the window, horror in her eyes as the reality dawned on her too. She jumped from her seat and caught my shoulders. "We'll figure something out. We'll work a vanishing spell." She stared at the kitchen where we could hear Bianca mumbling into her phone. "Or if we don't have enough power, I'll tell them it was me." Dot straightened her shoulders as somebody pounded on the door of the coffee shop. "Yes, that's the right thing. I'll tell them it was me."

Bianca appeared from behind the counter and started to walk toward the door. Her voice was sharp enough to cut ice. "Don't be such a fool all your life, Dorothy. If you tell them the truth, they'll lock you in a psychiatric facility and the witching council will eradicate you for treason." She shot a glare at her friend's small soft hands as she reached for the door handle. "And nobody is going to believe you snapped her neck with those trotters."

"And you don't have to be such a damn bitch all the

time." The words were out of my mouth before my brain registered them.

Bianca's lips curled to one side and she pulled the door open, standing back as Officer Fitzgerald burst into the room. He stared from Bianca, past Dot, and into my eyes with raised eyebrows. His voice was gentle as he crossed the room, holding out an arm to stop the two younger cops from approaching me. I tried not to stare at the scratches on their faces or the bright pink paint splattered all over their clothes. Great work, guys.

Officer Bert Fitzgerald cleared his throat. "Miss Jones, you know why I'm here." He took a step closer. "You're going to have to come with me, ma'am." He took another step forward and lowered his voice so that only I could hear him. "Unless you have something to tell me that might move the case in another direction." He tilted his head a fraction of an inch toward the old ladies.

Seconds ticked by like hours as I stared back at him. Of all the people I'd ever met, Officer Fitzgerald was the only one I knew who'd believe that Agatha had died at a witch's hand. My gaze slid over his shoulder onto Dot's hunched form and Bianca's frozen face. How could you unravel who was really to blame when every individual thread of the story was so tangled and worn? Virgil was right about hell; the descent was easier than swallowing a spoon of vegan ice-cream. I pushed myself to my feet and held my hands out for Officer

Fitzgerald to cuff me, but Bianca's voice slid across the room just as the metal grazed my wrists. "Officer, I think your phone is ringing."

Bert stepped away from me, reaching for his phone. He stared at. "No, it's not—" The phone began to ring in his hands and he pressed it to his ear, the lines on his forehead deepening with every passing second. "Sir, I don't understand, how can there have been an error?" He turned his back to the room. "I saw the autopsy report myself. I saw the photographic evidence, this is total fu—" He held his breath and screwed his face. When he spoke again his voice was as tight as a wire. "Understood." He shoved the phone into his pockets and gestured to the other two cops to leave. One of them started to argue, but Bert cut him down with a bark. "Get into the car, O' Malley. The case is closed. Orders from the top." He glanced at me as he crossed the floor, a silent exchange passing between us as we saw each other for what we were; two ordinary humans, caught in a supernatural web.

When he reached the door, he paused in front of Bianca and gave her a long, hard stare before dipping his head. "I'll be seeing you, Miss D'Arcy."

"Not if I see you first, Officer Fitzgerald." Bianca's lips were arranged in a pretty smile, but it was anything but innocent. The smile a lion might give its prey. She slammed the door in his face and said to nobody in particular. "Oh dear, my fingers must have slipped."

I folded my arms over my chest as I crossed the floor to stand in front of the old women. I wasn't sure exactly what I should say. Was it necessary to thank somebody for saving you from a conviction they tried to land on you? I exhaled and met Bianca's eye. "Thank you, for whatever you did there. I appreciate it."

"I didn't do it for you," Bianca snapped. "I did it to protect the coven, and the leyline, and the witching world, and every other thing I spent a hundred years fighting for."

"Okey-dokey…" I turned my back on Bianca and faced Dot. "What you were trying to do was kind, Dot. It was an accident. I think Agatha will understand that."

"You've seen her?" Bianca was suddenly in front of me, both of the old women's faces sharp as they studied me.

I imagined Tom's voice in my mind, warning me to be cautious. Look out for thin ice, Priscilla Jones. I scrunched my face up and gave a laugh. "Please! I've seen the spell books, I've seen Agatha's albums and her paper cuttings, so witches, I believe in. Ghosts?"

Bianca's laugh was the tinkle of ice in a crystal glass. "Well, you'd never know with dear Agatha, would you?" Her voice was razor-sharp. "She must have had such a lot of unfinished business…" The bell above the coffee-shop door rang out cheerily as she pulled the door open for me.

I stepped over the threshold, nodding at Dot, when a

thought struck me. I glanced at the two women. "That report on Officer Bert's desk?" I asked. A look of genuine confusion crossed over both faces and I shook my head. "Nothing, doesn't matter."

As I stepped onto the pavement, Bianca's voice followed me into the night. "We'll be seeing you, dear. Take care of your secrets. And ours." I had already reached the curb when her final words hit me. "Everything comes at a price."

CHAPTER TWENTY-EIGHT

I LEFT THE CAR AT THE BAKERY, PREFERRING TO WALK all the way home, and the fresh air helped soothe my stretched nerves. When I reached home, all sign of the earlier media storm had vanished. Sadly, I couldn't say the same for the damage the cops had caused. As I stepped over the remains of my front door, I couldn't help but wonder who Bianca had spoken to on the phone. Somebody with the power to make a murder case vanish without a trace. An order from the top, Bert had said. City Hall? The President? A criminal? My mind whirled with thoughts of who my mysterious savior could be. And whether or not I wanted to be in their debt.

"She's back, she's back, she's back!" Muffin was the first to come thundering down the stairs, his ginger tail swinging, followed by Tom and Pussy, who arrived at my feet in a jumble of claws and hair.

I reached down to pet them, but I was distracted by the shimmer of Agatha passing over and back through the walls of the hallway above. I looked down at the cats. "Give me five minutes, okay? I promise I'll tell you everything, but I need to talk to Agatha first."

Yowls of protest followed me up the stairs, but they let me go. I found Agatha in her study, staring at the paper cutting from 1895. I slid silently into one of the two leather armchairs. "How much do you know, Agatha?"

The ghost gave me a crooked smile. "About as much as you do. I was hiding in your hair until you left the coffee shop."

"What the hell?" I ran my hands through my hair, staring at her. "You're joking, right?"

Agatha reached out and touched the jeweled barrette she slid into my hair the night before. "To quote a very annoying girl I once knew, 'Nope, nope, nopety-nope'."

"You're the worst boss I've ever had, I just want you to know that," I said. Agatha mimicked me, repeating the words in a whiny, high-pitched voice. I stuck my tongue out at her and she made a farting noise. I let out an exasperated laugh and she turned back to her newspaper clippings. "How are you doing, Aggy? Really? It must have been hard to hear those things."

"I'd forgotten my mother's face, you know. Until

tonight, listening to them tell my story. I never forgot that voice, but her face…" Her words were so unexpected that I froze. She didn't lift her eyes from the desk. "Bianca was right, you know, when she said I had a lot of unfinished business." Her smile was the very mockery of happiness; sorrow carved in flesh. "I thought when I found out how I'd died, that everything else would come flooding back, but that's not how it works, is it?" She met my eye for the first time. "I'm going to have to resolve all of my unfinished business, one sorry tale at a time. And I'm not going to like every memory that returns."

I pressed my hands to my lips and stared back at her. One-hundred-and-thirty-nine year's worth of mistakes and agonies and joys. "We'll take it one bridge at a time, Agatha, but we'll get there. You've got the world's best assistant and the world's most handsome familiars in your corner." I glanced at the box again and took a deep breath. "You brought all of us here for some reason, Agatha. We just have to figure out what it is."

Agatha rolled her eyes as the sound of claws tapping on the floorboard outside the door grew louder. She waved her hand. "Go on, shoo, out you go to your little hussy harem."

"They're not my harem," I insisted, slinking across the floor.

"Whatever, hipster hussy," the ghost retorted. As I opened the door something flew over my shoulder, barely missing my nose, and landed on the floor between the cats.

Pussy was the first to recognize what it was and he purred up at me with a feline leer. "It's your lucky day, Pricetag. Extra-large and ribbed for her pleasure." Agatha cackled softly on the other side of the door and Pussy's smug grin widened. "See, I always told you I was her favorite."

"Great, Pussy. You stay with ghost granny, while the rest of us of chill out on the couch, okay, little pussy-wussy?" I crooned. Pussy was the first to make it to the living room. I collapsed on the couch, and I stroked each cat in turn. I grinned at the pile of blankets waiting on the floor. Finn passed them out so that everyone was covered without a single screech from my mouth. And so what if I was a little bit disappointed not to catch a single glimpse of a buttock or anything more interesting, I was only human.

Tom settled himself on my left, and Pussy and Finn slouched down to my right. I swiveled so that I was lying across them, my head in Tom's lap, my thighs over Finn's, and my feet resting just on Pussy's hip. I closed my eyes as Tom began to stroke my hair from my forehead, recounting every detail of the night since I'd last seen them. I felt Tom tense when I repeated Bianca's words. "That old bitch." I tried to headbutt his stomach and he grinned. "What? She is an old bitch. You were right not to tell her about Agatha or us. We haven't seen the last of that sly dog." He flicked my nose gently. "By the way, if you want to nuzzle me with your head, you should aim a bit lower next time."

Before I could respond to Tom, or bite him, Pussy drawled, "Yeah, if you're taking suggestions, I've got an itch you could probably scratch with those delightful little feet. Just move them a little to the right..."

I swung myself back into a seated position, ignoring Tom and Pussy's protests, and looked at Finn. My sweet ginger muffin, at least I could trust him not to lower the tone. He raised his hands in the air. "Hey, don't look me, I don't have any demands." I smiled and leaned back into the sofa, resting my head on his shoulder. "Although, I do remember you suggesting something about Sex on the—"

My back-handed slap left the imprint of my fingers on his abdomen and I gave the three of them a warning glare. "If anyone says anything about rubbing him better, I'm going to shove Agatha's broomstick up their ass."

Pussy pressed his lips together and stared at the floor like he was going to explode. I couldn't suppress my grin. "Say it. Whatever smart remark you have about broomstick violation, just say it."

"Kinky." He spat the word out and released a breath, his whole body relaxing visibly.

I shook my head and patted him on the knee. "If we

ever find a way to stop you from randomly turning into a cat, I'm sending you for therapy for that."

Finn lifted one eyebrow and put on a deep voice. "When dirty talk, goes bad."

Tom smirked and reached for the remote control. "Hey, maybe it's on right now."

The television screen in the corner shuddered into life. And a wide smile spread across my face as I closed my eyes and settled deep into the couch. I was content, for the first time in a long time. Between the whole mess with dickhead back in Portland, and the murder investigation, I had to admit I was starting to think my life would never be normal again. Not that lying on a couch with three naked cat men shifter things was normal, but I would take what I could get.

"Can we get you anything?" Tom asked, turning slightly to face me as he rested his tattooed arm on the couch behind my neck. "Wine? Coffee? Tea? Are you hungry?"

"No, I'm fine. I have everything I need right here." I smiled sleepily at him and turned to look at the other two. "I'm not going to get all emotional on you, but I want to say thanks. For taking care of the cops so I could escape, and knowing I'd forget my keys, and not telling me I snore. And not licking me. Because cat's tongues are really weird. Like tiny pink bits of sandpaper." The three men exchanged a look and I held my hands up. "No, I mean it. Thank you, Tom, and

Finn, and—" I stopped short. "Okay, seriously. You're going to have to tell me your real freaking name, because I can't keep referring to you by that…word."

Pussy grinned, leaning back and closing his eyes. "Poor little Pricetag. I guess that's just one more mystery you'll have to save for another day."

I groaned, rolling my eyes. Yeah, the mysteries were really piling up in Salem.

Accepting defeat for now, I closed my eyes and gently fell into a deep, peaceful sleep, surrounded by the presence of the three comforting strong men who had proven themselves to care more for me than anyone else in my life ever had.

It was a strange life; not the one I expected to have. But it was mine. And I would hold onto it with all the power in my being.

ABOUT L.C. HIBBETT

L.C. Hibbett is an author from Ireland who is obsessed with reading, writing, romance, mystery, and magic. Since she began publishing, L.C.'s husband has begun to find it difficult to differentiate between her pajamas and her outside clothes and her children have decided to forgo clothes entirely. Except for underwear--L.C. is steadfast in her insistence that everyone wear knickers on the trampoline. I think that tells you everything you need to know...

If you would like sneak peeks of L.C.'s upcoming books and notifications of her super-secret release day sales for her loyal readers, head to lchibbett.com and sign-up to receive her Newsletter updates.

Find L.C. Hibbett online:

www.lchibbett.com

ABOUT N.M. HOWELL

N.M. Howell is an author, publisher, and all-around nerd from the West Coast of Canada. She has an obsession with coffee, spicy food, and the rain, and she absolutely hates sleeves. (Seriously, they're like little fabric prisons!) When not working on her latest book - or latest ten books, more realistically - she spends her time wandering the world and fighting with her micro-wolf pup over who gets the best spot on the couch. Hint: the dog wins.

Find N.M. Howell online:
www.nmhowell.com

Made in the USA
Monee, IL
01 August 2020

37365417R00152